the
bag
MAN

RANDALL CALDWELL

the bag MAN

a fifteen-day revelation

TATE PUBLISHING
AND **ENTERPRISES**, LLC

Scriptures taken from the *Holy Bible, New International Version*©, NIV®. Copyright © 1973, 1978, 1984 by Biblica, Inc.© Used by permission of Zondervan. All rights reserved worldwide. www.zondervan.com©.

This novel is a work of fiction. Names, descriptions, entities, and incidents included in the story are products of the author's imagination. Any resemblance to actual persons, events, and entities is entirely coincidental.

The opinions expressed by the author are not necessarily those of Tate Publishing, LLC.

Published by Tate Publishing & Enterprises, LLC
127 E. Trade Center Terrace | Mustang, Oklahoma 73064 USA
1.888.361.9473 | www.tatepublishing.com

Tate Publishing is committed to excellence in the publishing industry. The company reflects the philosophy established by the founders, based on Psalm 68:11,
"The Lord gave the word and great was the company of those who published it."

Book design copyright © 2011 by Tate Publishing, LLC. All rights reserved.
Cover design by Kellie Vincent
Interior design by Lindsay B. Behrens

Published in the United States of America

ISBN: 978-1-61346-504-2
Fiction / Christian / General
11.09.27

I want to dedicate this book to my parents, Everett and Lillie Caldwell, who raised me the correct way according to the Bible. I learned more from you than anyone else what true ministry really is. I also want to say thank you to my wife, Jerrie, who believed I could do anything I wanted to and put up with me while doing so. You guys are my inspiration!

prologue

Another man got there a little sooner than I did. When I got there the other guy had all ready turned the body over. He put his fingers to the woman's throat to see if she had a pulse. She was barely alive. I assumed that he was a doctor or someone who had medical training. I could see the knife sticking out of her chest as she lay on her back. I had my sweat towel in my pocket, so I got it out. I tried to put it around the wound, but the other man pushed it away. I got out my cell phone and called 911. As I was explaining what happened, the other man reached up and grabbed the knife that was sticking out of the woman's chest. He was trying to pull it out. I grabbed the man's hands and tried to stop him, yelling, "Don't pull it out. She'll bleed to death before help can get here!" He grabbed me and quickly shoved me away, leaving blood stains on my shirt. He turned his head and looked into my eyes. It was then that I realized who the other man was ...

day

ONE

THE BEGINNING

I live in the small town of Dullsville. Nothing special ever happens in Dullsville. We have our regular businesses, our regular restaurants, our regular events, and regular people. On the square we have a nice fountain and benches for people to sit down on. At night the lights shine on the fountain, and it looks great. During special events they even change the color of the water in the fountain. On occasion, they put up a large screen and have outdoor movies for the people free of charge. Other than that, nothing out of the ordinary ever happens.

Don't get me wrong, I love living in Dullsville. Most of the people are nice enough, and there is a big variety of food establishments to choose from. We even have a Walmart to shop at. There is a boatload of good churches to choose from, and we have a very good school system for the kids. All in all, Dullsville is a good place to live, and I am happy that I live there. But sometimes it can get a little routine and repetitive.

One spring night all of that changed for me. It was mid-May, and I just wanted to do something other than my normal routine for the evening. I decided to get in my car and drive up to the square and walk around for exercise. Other than driving through the square, I really never had stopped to enjoy the scenery it provided. I have lived here for four years, so I figured it was about time to enjoy some of the fruit from my tax dollars. Yes, tonight would be different for me!

I parked on the corner and walked around the square for a little while, enjoying all the scenery and doing a little window shopping. While I was walking around enjoying myself, I kept hearing what sounded like a man singing in a very soft voice, but I couldn't tell where it came from. I kept wondering to myself, *Is someone singing into a microphone or a speaker of some kind?* I just couldn't figure out where it was coming from. So at that point I paid it no attention. After walking around a few minutes, I decided to sit down on a bench in front of the fountain. It was a beautiful sight! It had one big water spout in the middle with small spouts all the way around it. It was very hypnotizing with its eurhythmic, pulsating sprays. I had finished my walking for the day and was sitting there relaxing before I had to leave for the night.

As I continued sitting there, I started to hear that soft male voice singing again. It seemed to be getting closer by the minute. As it continued to get louder I looked around to see if I could finally see where it was coming from. To my surprise, it was actually a person. Out of nowhere this gentleman came walking by. As he got closer to me I could start to make out what he was singing. It wasn't anything I had heard before, but it was pleasant sounding and actually in tune. He kept singing this same phrase over and over, "I am the Bag Man; the Bag Man I am he. Come see the Bag Man, and see what you can be."

The gentleman was very nice looking and appeared to be in his late twenties. He wore a suit and he was carrying a duffel bag on his shoulder. As he walked by me, he was just singing without any care of what people thought about it. He paid no attention to me as he passed by. I turned my head away so as not to appear too nosey about his business. When I turned my head back to look at him again, he was gone. I looked around, but I didn't see him anywhere. I thought, *Huh, that was weird.*

Before I could even get that thought out of my head, I heard the singing again. It was the same guy coming from the same direction as before. It was like déjà vu, only different. This time the guy was looking directly at me. Every step he took, he had his eyes fixed on me. When he got to where I was sitting, he hesitated for a split second and looked into my eyes. It felt like his eyes were piercing my soul to the very core! Then, as quickly as he walked up to me, he walked away, still singing that same song and still looking back at me.

The next thing I remember is pulling my car into my driveway. I turned the car off and just sat there for a couple of minutes while I collected my thoughts. *Was what I just witnessed real, or did I just imagine it? How did I get home? I just don't remember! Maybe I'm just tired and need some rest.*

When I got inside I kissed my wife and headed for the shower. The hot water beating down on my shoulders was so relaxing. It was exactly what I needed. By the time I got out of the shower, I had forgotten all about the guy on the square and was back to my old self again. That night when I went to bed, I fell asleep as soon as my head hit the pillow.

day

TWO

When I woke the next morning, I was refreshed from a good night's sleep. I hadn't slept that well in a long time. I guess the walk and jog did me some good after all. Maybe I should do it again, what could it hurt?

When I got off of work I was so tired. The day was extremely busy, and I was stressed to the max from dealing with so many complaints from so many customers. I was having second thoughts about going to the square to do my walking for the day, but I have always heard that you have to break into the habit of going. Once you get started, it's easier to maintain the habit, but the hard part is getting started. So I made myself go.

I parked in the same parking spot on the side of the square. Once I had completed my stretching, I started my walking. My goal was to walk five miles a day. It was a goal that I had to work up to slowly. After the first mile I was already winded and needed to take a break. While I was sitting on the bench next to the fountain, a young lady came and sat down on a bench that was facing me. I couldn't help but notice her because she was so attractive and was dressed very nicely. There wasn't a single blonde hair out of place. Her makeup complemented the natural beauty and texture of her face. When she turned a certain way, I saw the sparkles from the diamond necklace that was around her neck and hanging ever so close to the top of her dress. Her dress was made of a nice material. It was a classy dress that hung nicely down to her knees and showed the perfect amount of cleavage on top. Her fingernails were manicured and had white tips on them. Her shoes looked like they cost more than my entire closet! Even the way she sat on the bench showed a well-trained and proper lady. It was obvious to me that she lived a life of prosperity. She had it all: hair, clothes, jewelry, and a nice shape to her body. She could literally be classified as the perfect-looking woman.

After she had been there a few minutes, I could hear her as she started to cry. She was trying to hide it but was unsuccessful. I didn't know what to do. I didn't have much experience in talking with people about their problems, so I just sat back and waited for her to say something first, but she never did. I knew that I should have tried to help her, but what could I do? Who was I? I was just a regular guy; I was nobody special. I felt bad for her, but it was none of my business. I couldn't take much more crying, I have never responded well to women crying, so I decided to get up and jog for a while.

As I was jogging and waiting for the traffic light to change on the square (you have to keep moving so your muscles won't cool down), I noticed someone standing across the street on the other side. He kept staring at me the whole time I was there. When the light turned green he just stood there as I passed by him. He never once took his eyes off of me and had an agitated look on his face. It was then that I recognized the man. I didn't know his name, but it was the same guy from the night before. He was the guy that was singing that song I told you about, "I am the Bag Man..." He had on the same clothes and carried that same bag on his shoulder. When I turned to get a better look at him, he was gone. I don't want to sound crazy here, but he just disappeared! It was spooky!

It's amazing what you see when you just walk or jog around. Most people pay you no attention. They just carry on with their tasks at hand. It's crazy what people do when they think no one is watching them. But on this day I think it was a two-way street. I was watching, and I was being watched!

I followed the same path as the night before. I heard people laughing and shouting as I passed by them on the street. Through the windows of the restaurants as I passed by, I saw normal people out having a good time. Even the kids were laughing and playing. I could even see my own reflection in the windows of the businesses as I went by them. It's amazing how much I looked like my father.

Even with all of this going on around me I couldn't keep my mind from going back to the lady on the bench. I should have approached her to see if she needed help, but I didn't. I was afraid that I couldn't help her. It was obvious she was from a different class of society than I. How in the world could I help her? These questions pounded in my head as I kept a steady pace with my jogging.

When my jogging brought me back to the same location where the benches were at the fountain, I was surprised and intrigued by what I saw. There was that "Bag Man" again, only this time he was kneeling down in front of that same lady sitting on the bench. I wondered, *What could this guy be saying to her?* As I jogged by them my pace slowed slightly so I could see what was happening, but I just couldn't make out what he was saying to her. The whole time he was talking, though, the lady's eyes were shedding tears that ran down her face and cheeks. The Bag Man turned his eyes slightly toward me and then back again to the lady. I think he just wanted me to know that he knew I was there.

At that point I just jogged repeatedly around the fountain itself so I could see what was happening without being so obvious. The third time around the fountain I saw the Bag Man reach deep into that bag he had on his shoulder. He pulled out a white handkerchief and started wiping the tears from the lady's cheeks. The lady reached up and took the handkerchief from the Bag Man's hand and began to wipe the tears from her eyes. She folded it in half and buried her face deep into it for a couple of minutes. The whole time, the Bag Man never once stopped talking to her. When I made my way back around to them the lady removed the handkerchief from her face. Her face suddenly started to glow with joy. It literally beamed with excitement. They stood to their feet and the lady gave him a quick hug and said, "Thank you." She turned and walked away with almost a skip in her step.

What happened next was a puzzle to me. The Bag Man sat down on the bench and he buried his face into the same handkerchief that the lady had used. I watched as his body began to shake a little and then more by the second. When he removed the handkerchief from his face, I saw that he was crying himself. The tears were flowing from his eyes and down his cheeks. He had black streaks on his face. Then it hit me! Everything the lady had on her face was now on the Bag Man's face; the handkerchief somehow transferred it to his face. At that point the Bag Man began to cry uncontrollably. He suddenly got up and began to run away. I didn't know what to do, so I chased after him to find out what was going on.

When he reached the corner of the building, he turned and ran down the side street. I followed behind him, but when I turned the corner he was nowhere to be found. He had disappeared into the darkness of the night.

With a hundred questions running through my head, I turned and walked back to my car. I just sat there for a minute and pondered the questions in my head, looking for answers. I couldn't come up with a reasonable explanation of what had just happened.

So I went home, took a shower, and went to bed. My wife asked me if anything was wrong. "No," I said, "just tired."

For some reason, I just couldn't sleep well that night. The Bag Man and the events that happened on the square kept coming to mind. It wasn't that big of a deal, and it didn't even involve me, but for some reason it had an effect on me.

day

THREE

When I awakened the next morning, it was difficult to get out of bed. I was still tired from not sleeping properly and was perplexed about the events I had witnessed the night before. My wife asked me if I was all right, and I simply responded with, "I'm fine. My body is still adjusting to the new exercising I am doing. I'm fine." Deep down in my heart I knew there was more to it than that, but I didn't even know myself what it was.

I got up as usual and helped myself to a large cup of coffee. After that I was more like my old self again. After a long hot shower and getting dressed for work, I was fully awake. A good hot breakfast always helps too. As I was leaving for work I couldn't help but see the concern on my wife's face. She could somehow tell something was churning deep down inside of me, even if I couldn't see it myself. With a smile and a kiss goodbye, she said nothing about it. Not that it would do any good. I can be a stubborn man.

When I left work that day I knew that I was stressed and knew I needed to get rid of some of it before I went home, so off to the square I went.

When I started my run for the evening, I ran with a purpose. I was more focused on running than usual. My mind wasn't thinking about anything at all except for running. It felt great! I wasn't a great deal winded despite the fact that I hadn't even taken a break to rest. I just let my mind wander and escape the stress of the day. It didn't take long to complete my run. I ran with passion and vigor. I felt energized and yet also felt relaxed at the same time. It must have been a breakthrough with my exercising. I had always heard that if you stick with it, you would start to feel different about yourself. At that moment, I felt good about myself.

I was on my way back to my car when I heard loud screaming from the other side of the square. I looked in that direction and noticed that the Bag Man was also standing off to the side watching the incident. Then my attention was drawn back in the direction of the people doing the screaming. It was two men and a lady doing the yelling. One man was tall and looked to be in his early fifties. The other man, who was doing most of the yelling, appeared to be in his thirties. The lady looked to be about the same age as the younger man.

From what I could gather from the yelling, the lady was the younger man's wife, and the older guy was the father of the younger man. The father was trying to explain something to the son, but the son kept interrupting him. It was obvious that the son didn't want to hear what he had to say. All he wanted to do was cuss his father out. The son was becoming more and more aggressive and in his father's face. The father was now starting to give it right back to the son. They were both in each other's face yelling at each other. The wife was trying her best to break it up but wasn't having much luck. The father was yelling at the son, and the son was cursing the father, and the lady was now screaming at both of them. People were starting to gather around to see what was going on. I heard someone in the crowd say that the police were on their way.

Then, suddenly, something weird happened. The Bag Man quietly walked up to the two men arguing and sat his big bag down on the bench next to them. At that point he still hadn't said anything yet. While the old man was talking to his son, the Bag Man opened up his bag and proceeded to take something out of it. I couldn't tell what it was at first because it was folded up, but when he unfolded it I could tell it was a baseball cap of some kind.

While the old man was still talking, the Bag Man walked up behind him and in one swift motion put the baseball cap on top of the old man's head. The old man stopped talking for a brief second and turned to look at the Bag Man. The old man quickly snatched the hat off of his head and threw it on the ground saying, "I don't want this. It's not mine. Leave me alone!" The Bag Man just shrugged his shoulders, picked the hat up, and walked off. The old man continued snapping at his son.

The Bag Man walked around the fountain and came up behind the younger man and put the hat on his head also. The young man jerked it off of his head and threw it directly at the Bag Man, hitting him in the chest and said, "What the #%&* are you doing? Go away! Get out of here before you get hurt!" The Bag Man just picked up the hat from the ground, went to the bench where his bag was and sat down holding the baseball cap in his hands.

At that point the two men had calmed down a little because a police officer drove up and got out of the patrol car. I recognized the officer. It was Officer Smith of the Dullsville Police Department. She was a compassionate and nice person but could get very tough and aggressive if needed. I slowly made my way a little closer because they weren't yelling anymore and I couldn't hear them. I wanted to know what they were saying. I guess I was being a little nosey.

When I got close enough to hear what they were saying, the officer was explaining that she had received a call that they were disturbing the peace and they had to stop or be cited for public disturbance. The young man started yelling again at the old man as he was explaining the situation.

Officer Smith interrupted him, "Sir, I already told you once to calm down and get control of yourself. I have been courteous and respectful to you so far; I expect you to do the same. If you don't, I will handcuff you, put you in my patrol car, and take you to the station and book you for disorderly conduct and obstruction of a police investigation. Do you understand?"

The young man's wife stepped forward and said, "He understands. It won't happen again." The wife pulled him aside and started reasoning with him to stay in control of his emotions.

Meanwhile, Officer Smith gathered information from the old man and ran background checks on everybody. Everything came back clean. The officer told the two men that they needed to work things out when everyone was calm and in an orderly fashion. She suggested that they have other people with them to act as mediators for the two of them. She also told them to do it in private and not in public. The officer then sent them on their way in two different directions.

As they were walking away the old man turned around and said, "I love you, son."

The young man turned around to face his father and replied, "Well, I hate you!" His wife put her arm in his and pulled him away saying, "Let's go." With that statement, everyone walked away, including the officer.

Everything was now peaceful again and order had been restored thanks to Officer Smith. Then I noticed that the Bag Man was still sitting on the bench, still holding that hat in his hands and looking up into the sky. He seemed to be preoccupied with something, so I looked up as well. But I didn't see anything. Then, suddenly, the Bag Man stood up but was now looking at the baseball cap in his hands with a puzzled look on his face, almost as if he was trying to decide what to do with the hat.

The Bag Man picked up his bag and put it on his back. Reluctantly he put the hat on his head and walked away. But he was different somehow. His body language was different. He didn't have that "get-up-and-go" in his step anymore. He was walking much slower than normal, and he was slouching his shoulders a bit. He also had a sad and mean look on his face. The few times I have seen him he was looking up and around, now he was looking down and away only to make eye contact when someone walked by him.

As the Bag Man walked away his countenance started to change even more with every passing second. Now, when someone walked past him he would slightly jump at them as if he was trying to scare them. People were crossing the street to avoid him.

Suddenly, he started walking very fast. I was behind him observing from a distance so I couldn't see his face, but I could see that both hands were balled up into fists as if he was ready to fight someone. Without warning he stopped in the middle of the sidewalk, looked up into the sky and started shouting for no reason, at least not one that I was aware of. He started walking again at an even faster pace. He started gritting his teeth and grinding them together. You know how people grit their teeth when they are really mad and want to fight? That was the way he was acting, very angry.

As he continued to walk his screaming became louder, and he started to jerk a little. He was acting as if he was possessed or something. He seemed as if he was arguing with himself, or another voice in his head maybe. What I was witnessing just didn't make any sense to me. Was he possessed? Was he on drugs? Maybe he was mentally handicapped and I just hadn't realized it yet. I just couldn't make sense of it all.

The Bag Man turned down the same side street as the night before and out of my sight, but I could still hear him screaming at the top of his lungs. I ran to the corner of the building to catch up with him, but before I reached the corner the screaming suddenly stopped. I turned down the side street and realized he was gone. He was nowhere to be found. Just like the night before.

As I was walking back to my car I wondered if someone was playing a sick joke on me. This really didn't happen, did it? I was now more confused than ever. My mind was racing in a hundred different directions trying to figure out what was going on. If this wasn't a sick joke, then who was the Bag Man, and what was he doing here in Dullsville?

day

FOUR

When I woke the next morning, I just stared at the ceiling for a few minutes trying to gather my thoughts for the day. My wife was already up making breakfast, so I had a little time to myself. I realized that this Bag Man stuff was starting to get into my head and I needed to clear a few things up about what I had seen over the last three days. So I decided that if I saw the Bag Man on the square that night I would approach him and get some answers. I was going to take control of the situation. I rolled out of bed and started to feel more excited about the rest of the day. Although, I must admit that the anticipation of getting answers later made it difficult to concentrate at work during the day.

After work I eagerly drove to the square and parked my car. As I started my jogging for the day I began looking around for the Bag Man. So far he always seemed to show up at the most unexpected times, almost as if he just appeared out of thin air. But this day I would get the jump on him. I was intent on finding him first, before anything else happened. Unfortunately, it didn't turn out like I had planned.

When I turned the corner and gained sight of the square, I saw the Bag Man already walking toward a lady sitting on one of the benches. The lady was just sitting there staring at the fountain as if she was in a trance or something. She looked like someone who had just had the worst day of her life. She had no movement or emotions. She literally looked dead on the inside, lifeless and alone.

I stopped my jogging and started stretching. Of course I was just doing that so I could watch the Bag Man, but I didn't want to be too obvious. Still, he knew I was there watching him. He made a point to make eye contact with me as if to encourage me to do so. I didn't need his encouragement though, somehow I felt compelled to watch him.

The Bag Man walked up to the bench and put his bag down. Then he sat down very close to the lady and put his arm around her shoulder. I thought it might be his wife or girlfriend, even though I had never seen him with anyone before. I guess it could have been a sister or relative of some kind. When he put his arm around her he softly laid her head on his shoulder. He still hadn't spoken a single word to her, nor she to him. They sat there motionless for what seemed like a very long time, but actually it was only about five minutes.

It was obvious that he knew I was watching, so I sat down on the bench on the opposite side of the square facing them and continued to watch. I could see enough to tell that he started talking into her ear. I could see his lips moving, but I was too far away to hear what he was saying. After a couple of minutes he moved her head from his shoulder and reached into his duffel bag and got out a very large book. He opened the book and found the page he was looking for and started to read to her. She turned and looked into the Bag Man's eyes and he then looked into hers. He no longer read from the book, but now he appeared to be quoting the book without even looking at it. I knew that look he had in his eyes. It was the same look he had when my eyes first made contact with his and they felt like they pierced my soul. He appeared to be looking into her soul as well, only deeper.

After a few minutes the Bag Man shut the book and gave it to her. Then he stood up, grabbed his bag, and walked away, leaving her there with the book. As he walked away, he walked toward me. I could see the lady on the bench behind him open the book and start to read. I thought this would be the perfect time to stop him and get a few answers to the questions that lingered in my head.

When he got close to me I stepped in front of him so he would stop. He simply side-stepped and went by me. As he walked by he looked at me. I took a deep breath and opened my mouth to ask him a question. Before I could even utter a sound he interrupted and said, "Not yet." He quickly turned his head away and continued walking, leaving me there speechless with my mouth still open. I thought that if he wouldn't answer my questions, maybe the lady on the bench would. I turned and looked in the direction of the bench, but the lady was no longer there. Turning back to the Bag Man, I saw that he was gone also. Now I was just plain *mad*! I talked with the people sitting on the other benches, and none of them remembered even seeing a man or woman sitting on that bench. Now I was mad and confused.

When I got home my wife quickly realized something was bothering me. This time she took the bold approach and confronted me about it. I tried to play it off as nothing but she wouldn't let up until I gave in to her questions. I started from the beginning and told her everything I had seen and everything that had happened over the last four days. I left nothing out. She sat there quietly and listened intently and carefully to every word that came out of my mouth. She said very little, and when she did speak it was only to ask a question. I could tell she was having a difficult time believing the whole story, but at the same time she could tell that I believed it.

After I finished telling her everything she just sat there silently for a few minutes. She had always done that when she was in deep thought about something. My wife was a wise woman, and she always chose her words carefully before she spoke them. This time she was silent for a longer period of time than normal. When she finally broke the silence she simply said, "I don't know who he is or what it has to do with you. Maybe you shouldn't go to the square tomorrow. Take a day off from your exercise and just rest. It might do you some good." She appeared to be concerned about how this was affecting me. I reassured her that there was no reason to be concerned and eventually I would figure things out. I headed for the shower. While in the shower I had time to ponder the subject and was actually feeling better about it. Maybe all I needed was to talk to someone and get it out of my system. It felt good to do that!

day

FIVE

It was Friday. With only one day left in the work week, I sure was glad I was off for the weekend. I needed the rest and the time away from the stress of work so that I could actually take a deep breath again. My day started as usual except I was running late. No breakfast that day, not enough time to stop! I basically hit the floor running. I hate doing that, but it happens sometimes. I guess it's a normal part of life.

The Bag Man never crossed my mind during the day because I was so busy playing catch-up at work. Before I knew it my day was almost done. Time sure does fly when you stay busy. My evening would not be any less busy because my wife made plans to cook dinner for some friends that night. If I was going to get any exercise in, it would have to be short and sweet. When I got off of work I got in my car and went to the square. I hit the pavement running. I was going for a quick run, then a shower and dinner. That was my plan for the night. At least, that is how I thought it would play out.

Before I could even get a good pace going, I saw the Bag Man walking on the opposite side of the square. I stopped running and sat down on one of the benches so that I could watch him and see what was going to happen. So far, something has always happened with him. What was it going to be today?

The Bag Man went to one of the benches and sat down. He reached into his bag and pulled out a bag full of bread scraps. He started breaking off little pieces and throwing them on the ground in front of him. After a couple of minutes, pigeons and other birds started to fly down and eat the pieces of bread. He started talking to the birds and some of them even ate from his hand.

I was so focused on what he was doing that I didn't even notice the guy in the wheelchair that pulled up next to him. The Bag Man looked at him and offered some of the bread to the guy. He took some of the bread and he too started feeding the birds. What I saw was two men feeding bread to the birds for almost ten minutes before either of them spoke a single word.

As they began to talk I could see their lips moving, but once again I wasn't close enough to hear what they were saying. The Bag Man pointed at the guy's legs. The other guy started rubbing his own legs. I could only conclude that they were talking about why he was in the wheelchair. The Bag Man listened intently as the guy told him his story. I could see the tears as they began to flow from his eyes as he talked. The Bag Man just sat there without saying anything in return. I thought it strange though that the Bag Man seemed to have somewhat of a smile on his face while the other guy was talking.

When the guy finished telling his story, the Bag Man asked him a couple of questions, and then he did something really, really weird. He got down on his knees in front of the wheelchair and pulled his bag down beside him. He looked into the guy's eyes one more time and said something to him. The guy nodded his head yes. The Bag Man reached down and pushed one of the guy's pants legs up as far as it would go. Then he pushed the other one up as well. I thought, *Why is he looking at the guy's legs?* Maybe there was a scar there or something, but I was too far away to tell.

What he did next was a little puzzling to me. I thought he was looking at the other guy's legs, but he was not. He reached into his bag and pulled out a large roll of some kind of material. The Bag Man unrolled it a little and started wrapping it around one of the guy's legs. The whole time he was doing that, he was steadily talking to the guy even though he only occasionally made eye contact with him. When he finished wrapping that leg he reached into his bag again and pulled out another roll and started wrapping the other leg. As I looked more closely I realized he was wrapping the guy's legs with bandages, you know, the kind that you wrap around a bad sprain or something like that.

No sooner did he finish wrapping the guy's second leg, he then started un-wrapping the guy's first leg. Then he started unwrapping the second leg. *Why was he doing that?* I wondered. *Why wrap someone's legs with bandages only to unwrap them a couple of minutes later? What good did that do when I've known people who wore them for weeks with little success?* After the Bag Man finished unwrapping the guy's legs he picked up the mangled bandages and put them in his bag. He sat back down on the bench and talked with the guy a few more minutes.

What I saw next literally sent chills running up and down my spine! The Bag Man stood up facing the guy as he held out his hands toward him. The guy grabbed hold of his hands and pulled himself up until he was in a standing position. The Bag Man suddenly let go of the guy's hands, leaving him there standing on his own power. The Bag Man took a couple of steps backwards away from him and motioned for him to walk to him. The guy struggled at first, but he made it. Then the Bag Man walked farther away from him and again made him walk to him. This time it was a little easier but still tough. The wheelchair guy was now beginning to walk on his own. I could see the enthusiasm on the guy's face start to grow. They repeated the process over and over and over again for at least twenty minutes, until he was comfortable walking on his own. The guy was so happy that he was jumping up and down and even had a little skip to his step.

The guy was crying tears of joy as he hugged the Bag Man tightly, showing his gratitude. The Bag Man was also crying. It was as if he were crying and laughing at the same time. The man thanked him one more time and then walked away, leaving his wheelchair behind. I could not believe what I saw! Was it a real miracle? I don't know, but it sure looked like one!

After wiping the tears from my own eyes, I looked at my watch and realized it was time for me to leave or I would be late for dinner. But I couldn't pull myself away just yet. My emotions were running wild, and I had to stay to see what was going to happen next.

The Bag Man then sat back down on the bench. He pulled up both pants legs as far as he could and grabbed the same bandages out of his bag that he previously used on the other guy a few minutes earlier. He then started wrapping those same bandages around his own legs. After he finished wrapping his legs he just sat there for a minute or two with his eyes closed. Then he stood to his feet. What happened next happened so fast that I didn't even have time to react to it. It was as if his legs quit working and couldn't hold him up anymore. He hit the ground with a hard thud! He pulled himself to a sitting position and just sat there on the ground looking as if he was trying to figure out what his next move would be.

I saw that he was having trouble as he was trying to drag himself with his arms over to the wheelchair at the other end of the bench. So I got up and quickly walked over to him and helped him get into the wheelchair. I asked him to explain what was happening to him, but all he would say was, "Thank you." He grabbed his bag and quickly rolled away in that wheelchair and out of my sight. I thought for sure that he would feel obligated to talk to me since I did help him, but he didn't see things my way.

I didn't know why I was feeling the way I did. I was happy yet sad at the same time. How could such a beautiful thing like a real-life miracle end with such tragedy? How could God let that happen?

When I pulled my car into the driveway I could see that our dinner guest had already arrived. I knew that I would get an earful from my wife for being so late for dinner. To my surprise she greeted me at the door with a kiss and a smile and said, "Welcome home, dear." Somehow she knew it would happen. I guess my wife was used to it by now because she never mentioned me being late for dinner. Dinner went well even though I was preoccupied with thoughts about the Bag Man.

day

SIX

We slept late because it was Saturday and last night's dinner party lasted well into the late evening. It was almost midnight before we actually got to bed. We were both extremely tired, me from my stress and my wife from working and putting together last night's events. The clock showed that it was 8:12 a.m., and my wife was still fast asleep. I got dressed quietly, made my coffee, and went to the square for my exercise. My thoughts were to finish running and get home as soon as possible so my wife and I could spend the rest of the day together. Because of our lifestyles, jobs, and kids, we don't get to spend a lot of time alone together. I thought it would be nice to do so for a change.

For some unknown reason I felt like doing things differently. On the way to the square I drove down different roads. I was going to park in a different spot and even run a different route this time. I guess I thought it would take away the feeling you get when you do something over and over again the same old way. The feeling of being stuck in a rut is what I'm talking about. Maybe doing things differently would give me more motivation about my exercising.

When I drove around the square looking for a different place to park I was already in deep concentration about where I was going to run. Without warning a child, who looked to be about twelve years old, stepped out into the crosswalk in front of me. Instinctively, I slammed on my breaks as hard as I could and turned the steering wheel. The boy then realized he was about to be hit and tried to jump out of the way. When I finally got the car stopped, all I could see was the boy lying face down on the sidewalk. For a brief second I thought I had just struck and killed that boy. My heart sank deep into my gut like never before. I thought I was going to throw up. I could hear tires screeching behind me from the other cars slamming on their brakes so I dared not get out of the car until it stopped. What was only a few seconds seemed like an eternity wondering what had just happened.

When I was able to get out of my car I ran over to the boy. He was huddled up into a fetal position. I knelt down next to him to get a closer look. The boy opened his eyes and looked at me. Tears began to run down his cheeks. He was obviously scared.

"Are you all right," I asked. "Did I hit you with my car?"

The boy didn't respond. He just looked at me with a blank stare.

"Did I hit you? Are you all right?" I said.

Still I got no response from the boy. Maybe he was in shock.

A middle aged lady came running up to me.

"You didn't hit him," she said, looking from me to the boy and back at me again. "He jumped out of the way. You missed him."

What a relief that was! I looked down at the boy again and noticed the blood on his knees. He must have scraped them when he jumped out of the way.

"Are you sure you're all right, son?" I said again.

The boy got to his feet and slipped through my hands and started running away.

"Stop!" I yelled, but he just kept running.

"Strange," the lady said. "Well I guess he's all right then."

We briefly discussed what happened and exchanged information just in case I needed a witness.

When I finally got my car parked, I just sat there a few minutes. I was shaking so badly that I needed a little time to calm down and regain my composure. I think I was just as scared as the boy was.

While I was still sitting in my car, I saw the Bag Man walking across the square heading in a direction away from me. It was strange because he was not in the wheelchair that he left in the day before. In the distance I could see that little boy that I almost hit with my car walking in my direction. I wanted to get out of my car and go check on him, but my desire to watch the Bag Man was greater, so I remained in the car.

To my surprise, when their paths crossed and they were standing face to face, it appeared like they knew each other. A grown man and a boy were standing there together. *How do they know each other?* I wondered. *Is he a relative or just someone he knows?* I didn't know, but the boy seemed to be at ease with the Bag Man.

The Bag Man started doing something with his hands, but I couldn't see what it was because my view was from behind him. I got out of my car and walked around to the front of it to get a better view and leaned up against the hood. What I saw was unexpected. The Bag Man was using sign language. The boy would respond to him the same way. They were talking to each another in sign language. Suddenly I realized that's why the boy stepped out in front of my car. He was deaf and didn't hear me coming. That's why he ran from me, because he didn't know what I was saying. No wonder he was so afraid!

The two of them stood there talking in sign language for a few minutes. I reached into my car and got my cup of coffee and stood there sipping on it until they finished whatever they were talking about. They seemed to be carrying on a long conversation, but I had no clue what they were saying because I didn't have any real knowledge about signing. I've never really had a need for it or even thought about it. It was almost amazing watching the two of them sign because they were so good at it. I guess when you have no other option you learn quickly. All of those thoughts went through my head as I stood there waiting and watching.

When they finished their conversation the boy was standing in front of the Bag Man looking up at him and shaking his head yes. They walked over to one of the benches and sat down. The Bag man took his bag off of his shoulder and put it on the bench in between the two of them. He opened his bag and reached into it, moving things around like he was looking for something in particular. When he found what he was looking for he moved his bag so that he could sit closer to the boy. It was only after he moved his bag that I could see what was in his hands. I thought, *It's too hot for earmuffs. Why did he get those out?* Without delay he opened the set of earmuffs and put them on the boy's head, covering his ears.

After he put the earmuffs on the boy's head they started signing again. I could only reason that they were discussing why he put the earmuffs on the boy's ears. Their sign language conversation lasted about ten minutes and ended with the boy once again nodding his head yes. The Bag Man reached over and took the earmuffs off of the boy's ears and placed them on the bench next to him. The boy stood up and gave the Bag Man a high five hand slap. When the boy walked away, his eyes were wide open, and he had a big smile on his face. When the boy got out of his sight, the Bag Man picked up the earmuffs and put them on his head and over his own ears. He grabbed his bag and walked away slowly out of my sight.

I was still a little stressed from almost hitting that boy with my car earlier, so I started my stretching, which is what I always did before I started running. Running helped me to relax and free myself from stress.

After about ten minutes of running I was making my way back around to the square where I started when I saw the Bag Man going inside one of the businesses that was on the other side of the square. When I reached that business I stopped running and started stretching again. Of course I was looking in the window trying to see what was going on. I thought it strange because I had not yet seen the Bag Man more than once on any given day. Why was this day different?

The store he was in was the local mom-and-pop dollar store. When he got to the front of the store I saw him put a few basic items onto the counter to be paid for. It was simple hygiene items like a toothbrush, disposable razor, comb, wash cloth, and a bar of soap. Also he had selected a complete man's clothing outfit which included shoes, socks, undergarments, pants, belt, and a shirt. Nothing expensive or elaborate, mind you, after all it was a simple dollar store. But I suspect it was everything he needed. He carefully counted out the money and paid for it. The store clerk put everything into one large white bag and then the Bag Man left.

I didn't feel like running anymore, and wanted to get home to spend time with my wife, so I walked to my car and got ready to leave. As I circled the square to get back on the right road I saw the Bag Man walking from the side street. He seemed to be preoccupied with the things that he had just purchased from the store. Before I knew it he stepped out into the road in front of me. I slammed on my brakes and with a loud screeching noise was able to stop in time to keep from hitting him. I blew my horn repeatedly but he never looked up at me. He just kept walking. I positioned my car where I could pull up beside him. I rolled down my window and tried calling the guy but still got no response. I yelled at him as loud as I could, but still I was ignored. I had now reached the red light and had to stop. The Bag Man just kept on walking across the road, not paying any attention to anything but that bag. Thankfully there were no cars coming or he would have been hit for sure! He just kept walking with those stupid earmuffs over his ears.

When I opened the front door of my house I could smell bacon frying and pancakes cooking. It was a wonderful smell, and I was definitely ready to eat. I got a welcome home kiss and hit the shower as my wife continued cooking breakfast. She got to sleep late, so she was in great spirits. When I finished my shower the table was already set and waiting for me. As we started eating, we carried on normal chit-chat conversations for a few minutes.

"How was your running today, dear?" she asked just before putting a bite of food in her mouth.

"It was fine." I paused and took a sip of my coffee then continued.

"It was relaxing, yet, stressful at the same time."

"How so?" she asked as she fixed her eyes on me with a puzzled look on her face.

"You know, it's just the same old daily grind that you just have to deal with."

She continued without hesitating, "Did you see the Bag Man hanging around the square today?"

"Yea, I saw him."

"Tell me about it," she said as she sat her coffee cup down on the table.

I tried to pass it off as no big deal by saying, "You don't want to waste time listening to me talking about all of that stuff when we could be spending quality time together."

Elizabeth sat back in her chair and focused her gaze of fire upon me in a stare down. She crossed her arms and with a firm tone in her voice said, "Humor me. Tell me about it anyway, Peter!"

I knew that the day would come to a standstill unless I told her what happened. So I did just that. I told her everything that happened concerning the Bag Man and the boy.

When I finished telling her the story she sat there quietly, sipping on her cup of coffee. Finally, with an inquisitive look on her face, she spoke, "I find it strange that you saw the Bag Man on three different occasions on the same day. What do you think that means?"

I gave her a low grunt and said, "I have no idea."

I got up and started cleaning off the table and took the trash out as Elizabeth loaded the dish washer.

We carried on the rest of our day without any mention of the Bag Man, but he had definitely taken up residence in the back of my mind. Even if I didn't talk about it, I had realized that in a short period of time, this Bag Man had for some reason made me a part of his life, and I didn't know why.

day

SEVEN

After church today our small group home team went
out to eat lunch together. A home team is a small group
of people that get together a couple of times a month
or more and spend time together. It was not meant
to be something too spiritual like preaching or bible
study. That is something entirely different. This was
a group of people who wanted to create relationships
with other people. People who wanted to spend time
together and create friendships. People who wanted to
help each other in life. These are people who did life
together. My wife suggested that I tell the home team
about the Bag Man, but I didn't want other people
knowing just yet. Maybe I would tell them later.

After lunch, with my belly full, we went home.
I plopped down on the couch, turned the television
on, and took a good nap. I slept much longer than I
needed or wanted to. I try not to make a habit of it,
but you know how it is, sometimes it just happens that
way. We don't do much on Sundays anyway, it's usually a lazy day for us.

In spite of all of that I still wanted to get some exercise in for the day. I have noticed that it does make me feel better physically and mentally when I do. There might be something to this exercise thing after all. So I went to the square to run. It was about 7:00 p.m. in the evening, and the sun was well on its way to going down. The temperature was in the mid-seventies with few clouds in the sky. It was a perfect day to get some exercise.

I was about halfway through my run before I saw the Bag Man. He seemed a little different for some reason. His clothes appeared to be a little wrinkled and worn, and even a little dirty. I hadn't noticed that before. I also noticed that he had developed a distinct five-o'clock shadow, like he hadn't shaved in a couple of days. That seemed to make him look older than I originally thought he was. After watching him walk for a few seconds it was clear to me that he was now walking with a slight limp. Was that something new, or had I been so focused on what he was doing that I hadn't noticed before? The changes were slight in appearance, but they were there nonetheless.

I wanted to follow him, so I slowed my pace down from a run to a slow walk. I think he already knew that I would follow him. I also had the feeling that he literally waited for me to see him before he moved.

He walked off of the main road and down one of the side roads headed away from the square. He appeared to be looking for something. He made several turns onto other side streets and finally ended up in an alley behind some businesses. It was there that

I saw what he was looking for. There, at the end of the alley, was a parked car. He walked up to it and knocked on the window. After a couple of knocks the car door finally opened, and out stepped a large man. He was dirty and had clothes on that looked like old rags that I wouldn't even use to wash my car with. The Bag Man stood there and talked with the guy for a few minutes. I, of course, was too far away to tell what they were talking about. Toward the end of the conversation, the Bag Man took his duffel bag off his shoulder and opened it. He reached into it and pulled out a white plastic bag. I saw the logo on the side of the bag. It was from that dollar store that he had gone into the day before. He opened it up and showed the guy what was in it. It was the same items that he had purchased the day before. He put the items back into the bag and gave the bag to the large guy. The guy shook his head no, but the Bag Man insisted that he take it. He finally took the bag. They shook hands, and the Bag Man walked back down the alley toward me.

I wasn't sure if I should hide or just stand there and see what happened. I chose to just stand there leaning up against the side of the building. When the Bag Man got to the end of the alley where I was standing, I spoke first, "Is that your good deed for the day?"

He turned and looked directly into my eyes and said, "Watch and learn."

Then he just walked away. I thought he meant to watch the guy from the car, so I hung around the entrance of the alley to see what was going to happen. The guy just stood there at his car looking at the stuff in the plastic bag that he was given. Then he got into his car and started it. He backed out of the alley into the main street and drove off. I tried to run after the car, but I couldn't keep up with it. Finally I gave up and stopped chasing the car. I was out of breath and couldn't continue any farther. It was my one chance to see what was happening, and I blew it!

Frustrated, I walked to my car. On my way home I passed by a convenience store and gas station and saw the car from the alley, and the man was getting out of the car. Without thinking I pulled in and up to the gas pumps. I thought if I was going to watch I might as well get some gas while I was there. He went inside for a minute and came back out with a key. He went to his car and got the plastic bag that the Bag Man had given him. He went to the bathroom door and unlocked it with the key he had gotten. I finished pumping and paid for my gas and pulled my car to the other side of the parking lot, but close enough to still see when the man came out of the bathroom.

He was in there a good thirty minutes before he came out. He didn't look like the same guy that went in. He was clean-shaven and wearing new clothes. He took the key back to the attendant and got in his car and left. I tried to follow him, but the traffic was so heavy that I lost him. I went home not knowing what happened or who the man was.

That night I felt uneasy about myself. I even felt a little guilty because the Bag Man gave me a simple task to complete, "Watch and learn," and I failed to complete it. My wife finally convinced me that I was blaming myself for something that I had no control over. For my wife's sake I let it go. I didn't want her to worry about me. But deep down in my soul I knew that there was a connection between me and the Bag Man. I didn't know how or why, but my instincts told me it was there and I needed to find out what it was and what it meant. I decided from that point on I would be selective about what I told my wife. I wasn't going to hide anything from her, but I wasn't going to give her any reason to be worried about me unnecessarily. That task alone would prove to be more difficult than I ever imagined. Even though men generally don't want to admit it, wives tend to know more about their husbands than they do. It's true, whether we believe it or not!

day
EIGHT

It was Monday, and it felt like Monday all day long! It was strange how stressed and tired I was, considering I just had two days off from work. I guess it was the thoughts of getting back to the daily work grind. Yes, Mondays can be that way sometimes.

I had come to enjoy the benefits of running for exercise even though I had only been running for a week. I knew that I would need to run my stress away that evening. When I got off from work I changed my clothes and headed straight to the square for my run. I completed my usual stretches and hit the pavement running. Running made me feel relaxed. It gave me a sense of freedom. I could run as slow or as fast as I wanted. I could stop and go as I pleased, and I could think about anything and work it out as I ran. Running made me feel good about myself. When I felt that way, I felt like I could conquer the world if I needed to.

I stopped running before I got back to the square so I could cool down by walking the rest of the way.

When I reached the square I saw the Bag Man standing over on the sidewalk. I walked over to the fountain and sat down on the short brick wall that surrounded it. I reached my hands into the fountain and splashed my face with water to cool down more. I took the sweat towel that had been hanging from my neck and dipped it into the water and began to wipe my face to refresh myself with the cool water.

It was then that I heard a disturbance at the other end of the sidewalk away from the Bag Man. When I turned my head to see what was happening, I saw a restaurant owner pushing an older gentleman out the door of his business. He was shouting at him,

"Why don't you go find somewhere else to hang out? Go find somebody else to bother." the business owner said.

"But I like it here," the old man said.

"My customers are starting to complain about you. You are filthy, and you smell bad. You are running my customers away, and I'm loosing business because of you! Don't come back anymore!"

"I have no where else to go."

"That's not my problem. If you come back here again, I'll call the police."

The old man just walked away and found a quiet place to sit down and lean against a wall.

I turned my head to continue watching the Bag Man, but he was no longer standing in the same spot. When I looked back at the old man sitting against the wall, I saw the Bag Man standing there talking to him. It didn't surprise me that he was there. It was normal for him to do things like that.

After a minute of introductions, the Bag Man sat down next to the old gentleman. While they were talking, the Bag Man opened his bag and pulled a couple of things out of it and sat his bag over to the side out of the way. I could tell by the logo on the wrapper that it was a sandwich from the local Subway sandwich shop. He gave the sandwich and a bottle of Coke to the gentleman. The gentleman opened the sandwich and offered some to the Bag Man but he shook his head no. The Bag Man sat down next to him while he was eating and talked the whole time. Occasionally the gentleman would stop eating long enough to reply and get a drink of Coke. He even stopped every now and then to laugh at whatever the Bag Man was saying. It appeared as if they had known each other for a long time. When the gentleman finished eating his sandwich and drinking his drink, the Bag Man took the empty wrapper and empty bottle and put it back into his bag. I didn't know why he did that except there was no trash can around to put it in.

I guess I sat on the edge of the fountain a good twenty minutes watching them talk. They appeared to be talking like they had been best friends for years. I wondered if the Bag Man had known him before, maybe from his past. However they knew each other, they appeared to be comfortable sitting and talking together.

I didn't know how long they were going to sit there and talk, and my time to be home was quickly approaching. So I decided I would get up and walk over to them and introduce myself. I thought that if I did, they would invite me into their conversation and I could get a little information about the Bag Man. I leaned down to wet my towel one more time. About the same time I looked back up, the two men stood up and started walking away together. It was strange that they would do that at the very second I stood up. It was like the Bag Man knew what I was going to do before I did it. They walked at a slow pace as they continued their conversation. Still I just couldn't get close enough to hear what they were talking about.

As they walked around the corner, they walked beyond where I parked my car. As they kept walking I stopped at my car. The Bag Man slightly turned his body to look behind him. It was as if he was looking to see if I was going to follow them. I wasn't sure if he wanted me to or not, so I decided to stop following them. I got in my car and waited for them to get out of sight before I left.

It was obvious to me there was a strange connection between the Bag Man and me. Why else would he wait for me to be there before he does whatever it is that he does? I had this heavy feeling that I was supposed to learn something from him, but so far I hadn't figured out what it was. Deep down in my gut there was a gnawing feeling that I hadn't been able to get rid of. I didn't like not knowing!

day

NINE

A busy day at work helped to keep my focus on the job at hand. I didn't think about the Bag Man much because I just didn't have any free time to do so. I liked days like that because it made the day go by quicker. Before you knew it, your day was finished. Except today, it was busier than normal, so I had to work late.

I was in a rush when I left work. It was later than normal, and I needed to get my exercise in before it got dark. With a few quick stretches, off and running I went. I was feeling good. The night was a bit brisk, but for a runner who sweats a lot it was great running weather. It wasn't very busy where I was running. It was Tuesday night and not a lot goes on in town on Tuesday nights. I didn't have to worry about traffic much either. It was a great running experience, easy and flowing all the way through.

I finished my running and was taking my time as I walked to my car. I was hoping to see the Bag Man as I walked, but I did not. I got in my car and started it up. I was a little hesitant to drive away, still hoping to see him. Disappointed, I backed out of my parking space and pulled away. As I made my way around the square I noticed someone, a girl probably in her late teens, sitting on the edge of the fountain wall. She was sitting there crying. I felt uncomfortable about leaving her there by herself since it was getting dark, so I drove back around the square to check on her. Maybe it was my fatherly instinct coming out because I have a daughter of my own. Whatever it was kept me from leaving. When I came back around the square she was still there, only this time she had her face buried in her hands. Several people walked by her, and even stared at her, but no one stopped to see if she needed any help. I decided that I would stop and check on her, so I found a parking space as close as I could.

When I pulled into the parking space and turned off my car I spotted a shadow lurking in the background behind the girl. I opened my car door and was ready to jump into action as the shadow stepped out into the light. It was the Bag Man. I didn't think he saw me, so I quietly sat back down in my seat and pulled the door closed enough so that it would turn off the overhead light in my car. I sat there quietly and watched.

He was dressed in all black, and this time he was wearing an overcoat. I had never seen him with an overcoat before. He looked almost creepy. If I didn't know the guy, I would be suspicious of him because of his looks. He worked his way around to the front of the girl before he approached her. He was aware enough of her fear to approach her with caution. He spoke to her from a distance of about ten feet. It took him speaking a couple of times before the girl lifted her head and responded to him. Once she realized he wasn't a threat he moved closer and sat down next to her.

The night air had grown colder since the sun had gone down. The young girl was wearing only a sun dress and had started to shiver. The Bag Man took off his overcoat and placed it around the girl's shoulders. That seemed to calm her down a little.

They sat there on the edge of the fountain for a few minutes as the girl talked most of that time. He only interrupted her long enough to make a comment or ask a question. It was obvious to me that he, some-how, made the girl feel comfortable enough to talk to him, and when she started talking she told him everything.

After she finished talking, and had calmed down a bit, he began to talk. While he was talking, she began wiping the tears from her eyes. Whatever he was saying touched her so much that she became mes-merized by his words, almost like a hypnotic state of mind. When he finished talking, they just sat there for a minute. She looked like she was in deep thought. She looked at him and asked a question. He answered her question as they both stood up and walked away together.

I had no clue what her problem was and no idea what they had talked about, but I did know that there was more to it than met the eye. So I got out of my car and followed them from a distance. As they were walking together, it appeared that the Bag Man did most of the talking. They were walking very slowly as if time didn't matter. I found that pace to be irritatingly slow because I was used to a much faster pace of life.

After walking a few blocks, they finally arrived at the local drug store. I walked across the street and stood at the entrance of an alley so that I could stay out of sight and get a better view of where they were standing. They walked just inside the drug store. The front of the store was one large plate glass window, so I could see everything they were doing. They walked to an old pay phone inside the store. The Bag Man reached into his pocket and pulled out a handful of change and gave some to the girl. She hesitated at first, but after being reassured by him she took the change. She picked up the phone receiver and, with very shaky hands, put the money into the slot. She was shaking so much that the Bag Man dialed the number for her. As her lips started moving I could tell that someone answered her call. Suddenly, her other hand covered her eyes as she started crying. The Bag Man simply put his arm around her for support. After a few seconds she regained control of her emotions and began talking without trouble.

As she was talking on the phone, with her free hand she pulled the Bag Man's overcoat from her shoulders and gave it back to him. When she hung up the phone they went and stood at the entrance of the store. After a few minutes a nice black Volvo pulled into the parking lot. The Bag Man motioned for her to walk toward it. When the Volvo met the girl the back door opened. As she was getting inside the car she hesitated and turned to look at the Bag Man, but he wasn't there. She turned and looked throughout the parking lot, but he was nowhere to be found. She turned and slowly sat down in the backseat and shut the door. The car drove away.

I was so focused on what the girl was doing that I didn't realize the Bag Man had walked away. My first instinct was to run up the road and catch up to him, but I knew that would be useless. From my experience with the Bag Man so far, I had learned that when he leaves you won't find him.

The walk back to my car gave me some extra time to think about what had happened. I suppose there are many reasons why a teenage girl would get in the back of a car. Some were good and some not so good. But if the Bag Man was involved, I had a feeling it wasn't a bad thing.

When I arrived home dinner was already on the table and waiting for me. The kids had already eaten and were in their rooms doing their own things. My wife waited till I got home so she could eat dinner with me. While eating she asked me about my day, and about my visit to the square.

"How was your day dear?" she asked.

"It was very busy and hectic," I replied.

"Did you run into the Bag Man on the square this evening?"

"Yes, I did. He was there talking and walking with a young teenage girl for a while."

"Who was it?"

"I don't know."

"Do you think she knew him?"

Again I replied, "I don't know. It appeared like she didn't."

After a few moments of eating without talking, she started the conversation again.

"I've noticed that you are not as stressed tonight after seeing the Bag Man, as you usually are. Why is tonight different from all of the rest?"

I responded with a simple answer, "I don't know. Maybe I've gotten used to him."

As we were lying in bed that night, my wife snuggled up close to me and said, "I'm glad you're not so stressed tonight. I was getting a little worried about you."

"No need to," I responded. "I've got everything under control. I'm fine." Having said that, we fell asleep in each others arms.

day

TEN

When I awakened the next morning it felt like I had gotten the best sleep that I'd had in almost two weeks. It felt like all of my stress had melted away during the night. I reached over to give my wife a good morning kiss, but she wasn't there. Then I heard the noise in the kitchen and realized from the aroma that filled the air that she was cooking breakfast. I got out of bed and took a quick shower. My wife greeted me at the table with a wonderful breakfast and a passionate kiss. "Good morning," she said. We ate breakfast together and had a great conversation. When it was time to leave she walked me to the door and kissed me goodbye and said, "I love you."

My day at work went well. Nothing negative happened to speak of, and a lot of good things fell in place. I don't know why that day was any different from the rest, but somehow it was. It was the first time in quite a while that I felt like I had some control of my day. I can't explain it, but it felt really good.

When my work day ended I wanted to continue that feeling, so I went to the square for my daily exercise. When I parked my car, traffic was a bit heavy, and I wondered how productive my running would be, having to weave in and out of traffic a lot. It actually fell into good timing with the red lights and my running went smoothly.

On my walk back to the car I stopped at the fountain and wet my sweat towel so I could wipe my face off. While doing so, I saw the Bag Man walking on the sidewalk. When he reached the end of the sidewalk at the intersection of the road, he stopped. He slowly turned his head toward me and stared at me from a distance. He had no emotions, no gestures, and no words. He had a blank stare on his face. I didn't know how to respond, so I just stared back at him. He had never just stopped and stared at me before; it was kind of creepy. Yet I didn't feel threatened in any way. It even felt a little inviting. Then he turned and walked down a side street.

I couldn't let my day end like that, not knowing what was going to happen, so I followed him down the side street. I had to pick up my walking speed in order to keep up with him. He seemed like he was on a mission. I followed him down several streets into the backside of town, the side of town no one likes going to: the bad side of town. I was starting to feel a little concerned about our safety, but I continued to follow.

The Bag Man continued walking and quickly turned down a dark alley. I was about fifteen seconds behind him, so I had no idea what I was walking into.

When I turned the corner and regained sight of the Bag Man he was standing between a woman and a man. I heard shouting and vulgar language. I saw the woman fall to her knees and start begging for something, screaming, "Give it to me, please!" Then I realized the severity of the situation. We had stumbled into the middle of a drug deal! The woman on her knees continued to scream and tried to get around the Bag Man, but he once again moved between the man and the woman. The other man kept yelling vulgarities at both of them.

I was at the other end of the alley, and it was now dark outside. The only light was from a streetlight that was on a power pole above their heads, and it wasn't very bright. I could only make out faint facial features of the other man, and they weren't very clear. The Bag Man knew that I was close by, but the other people hadn't seen me yet. I was leaning against a building, watching the three of them, wondering what would happen next.

With every passing second the situation was getting louder and more serious, with the potential to turn violent very quickly. But the Bag Man wouldn't back down from him for a second. It was a side of him that I had never witnessed before, and that really made me nervous!

The woman had given up and was now flat on the ground weeping uncontrollably. The other guy tried to get to her by sidestepping the Bag Man, but again, he stopped him from getting to her. The man had taken all he could take and shoved the Bag Man out of the way. The Bag Man quickly stepped back into position and regained control. That made the other guy furious. He stepped back, and in one swift motion, pulled a gun from the back of his pants and pointed it directly at the Bag Man's forehead, close enough that the gun touched him. I thought he was dead for sure. The guy looked him in the eyes and said, "You've messed with the wrong guy. Now you're gonna pay!"

Before I knew it I reacted. I didn't think about it, it just happened. I screamed, "*Stop!*"

The guy turned to look in my direction as I stepped out into the light. Once he saw me, he panicked and ran away.

When I got to the other end of the alley the Bag Man was already kneeling down next to the woman. I helped him as he sat her up and leaned her against the wall. He sat down next to her. I was still standing, looking down at the Bag Man as he was trying to regain his composure. I asked him if he was all right, he just nodded his head yes as he took a deep breath. "I thought for sure he was going to kill you!" I said.

"Me too," he said.

After a brief moment of silence, I asked, "Do you know her?"

"I know of her," he said, as he wiped the sweat from his forehead. I didn't say it out loud, but I sure thought that was a big risk to take for someone you didn't know that well. He looked up at me and said, "I know you don't understand right now, but soon you will."

I'm usually calm and cool when things happen. Even emergency situations don't panic me too much. I usually act instead of reacting. I don't get nervous while other people are starting to freak out. It's after the fact when I start to realize how serious it was. That's when things affect me, but during the situation I am usually in control of my thoughts and emotions. This time it affected me way more than I expected. My hands were shaking, and my legs started to give out. I felt most of my strength leave my body, and I needed to sit down. I sat down against the wall opposite the Bag Man and leaned my head back and closed my eyes to rest for a minute.

After a moment of rest I heard the Bag Man moving around. When I opened my eyes he had put his arm around the woman and was holding her tightly against his side. With his other hand he pulled her head down against the front of his shoulder. She wasn't asleep, but she wasn't awake either. Her eyes were closed, but it seemed more like a trance of some kind rather than sleep. He sat that way for a few minutes until the woman started to moan a little. From what I could see of her facial expressions, it looked like she was in pain. The Bag Man started rocking back and forth, just like one would rock a baby back and forth. After a few seconds he began whispering things into her ear. For the first time I could actually hear what he was whispering. He was saying things like, "You're safe now. You're gonna be okay. I've got you. You can make it, I know you can." The Bag Man kept whispering those kinds of statements into her ear over and over.

I could see beads of sweat all over her forehead, and she was shaking uncontrollably from head to toe. I could tell she was having a hard time, and I too wanted to help. I still had my sweat towel draped around my neck, and remembered I had a bottle of water in my pocket. By now it was no longer cold, but it would help. I stood up and poured half of the water onto the towel, enough to wet it down. I went over and sat down on the other side of the woman and began to wipe her face off. The Bag Man stopped rocking long enough for me to do so, and then started back when I finished.

I don't know how long we sat there with her but every few minutes I would wipe her forehead and face as the Bag Man did his thing. We did this repeatedly until I used all of the bottled water. I could tell by the look on the Bag Man's face that he too was getting tired. I stood and said to him, "I'll be back in a few minutes."

I left and made my way to the closest business that was open and bought two more bottles of water. While I was there I called my wife to let her know what was going on so she wouldn't be worried. From the tone of her voice I could tell she was already concerned and told me to be careful.

I made my way back to the Bag Man and the woman. He was still rocking her back and forth and whispering into her ear. I opened one of the bottles of water and wet the towel again. What I did next I did on instinct and didn't really think about it much. I reached down and wiped the Bag Man's face clean to refresh him. I opened the other bottle of water and offered it to him to drink. He drank about half of it and gave it back to me. I put the top back on it and sat it down next to him and said, "It's yours." I folded the towel and laid it on the woman's forehead.

I looked at my watch earlier and saw that it was getting late. I knelt down on one knee so I could talk face-to-face with him. I reached into my wallet and pulled out one of my business cards and laid it on the ground next to his bottle of water. "My business card has my address and number on it. Call me if you need anything. I've got to go now."

He simply looked at me and gave me a nod of approval. As I was walking down the alley away from him he called to me, "Hey!" As I turned to look back at him he uttered two words, "Thank you." With that statement I turned and walked away.

On the walk back to my car, my thoughts became confused. I was happy that I got to see a side of the Bag Man that I hadn't seen before and to help him, but at the same time I felt a little ashamed and empty inside. I hadn't felt that way in years. I believed I did well by helping him, yet I should have done more. It was like a war going on inside my head. I couldn't reason in my mind why I felt that way, but the feeling was real and settled deep inside my stomach. My emotions and thoughts actually caused me physical pain. I had never felt that before, and I couldn't explain it away.

When I pulled into my driveway my wife and kids were getting out of the car. They had just arrived home from church. She walked immediately to me and kissed me. The look on her face showed concern for her husband. She whispered into my ear, "We need to talk." Even with only a whisper, I could tell she meant business, and it would be a serious conversation. The kids had their baths and went to bed.

I was watching the news when my wife entered the den with two glasses of iced tea. She sat one down on the coffee table and gave me the other one. She picked up the remote control and turned off the television. She sat down on the couch in a position that allowed her to face me directly. She paused and took a deep breath before she spoke. My wife was a woman of wisdom and always chose her words carefully before she spoke. I had never been a person who feared his wife, but the look on her face scared me a little.

I felt it necessary to start the conversation so that I could maintain control of how the conversation went.

"The expression on your face tells me that you are upset with me for some reason.

Are you?"

"No, I am not upset with you. But I am concerned about you."

"In what way?"

"I am concerned about you because I think you're hiding something from me about this Bag Man. You're not telling me the whole truth. I know you better than anyone on the planet, and I can tell when you're hiding something. I get defensive when you hide things from me. What are you not telling me?"

"I'm not intentionally trying to hide anything from you. It's just that I don't even understand what's happening. I'm having thoughts and emotions that I can't explain." I reached down and took a drink of tea to buy time to choose my words carefully. I learned that from her.

"You forget that I know you better than you know you. I'm your wife. I already know that about you. Talk to me!"

"For some reason I think I'm supposed to learn something from the Bag Man, but I can't seem to figure out what it is, and that frustrates me."

"You do this all the time. You over-analyze everything. You're thinking too much, and your brain is getting in the way."

"Well, I've never been accused of that before. You really think so?"

"I know so."

"How do I stop thinking so much? How do I keep my brain from getting in the way?"

"Let me help you."

"How do I do that?"

"Don't push me away. Open up to me instead. Let me inside. Let me experience it with you and we will figure it out together, husband and wife."

What she said to me made a lot of sense. So I told her everything that happened that night, except for the part involving the gun. I didn't think she needed to hear that part. It would have been too much for her to handle all at once. I wasn't trying to hide any-thing; I just didn't want her to suddenly panic about something that could have happened when it didn't happen. With that conversation I promised to make her a part of everything and for me to quit thinking so much. We ended the night on a positive note.

day

ELEVEN

It was Thursday, and my day started well. I slept like a baby all night long. It was the best sleep I'd had in a while. The sun was bright, and it was a beautiful day. My wife sent the kids off to school and was making me breakfast. What a wonderful woman! I didn't deserve to be treated like a king, but that's the way she treated me. She definitely was a gift from God! A quick shower and breakfast, and off to work I went.

My day wasn't very eventful, other than the normal stress accumulated throughout the day. So I basically had a typical day. But still, I wanted to get my normal evening exercise done. I changed my clothes at work as usual and went to my car. When I rounded the corner of the parking lot, there, leaning against my car, was the most beautiful woman I had ever seen. She was dressed in her jogging suit and was looking so fine! When I got closer to her, she walked toward me and softly embraced me. She gave me a soft gentle kiss. By the way, it was my wife.

"What a delightful surprise," I said.

"I wanted to get in shape also, and wanted to spend more time with you. I figured I would do both at the same time and exercise with you, if that's all right with you."

"Let me repeat myself, what a delightful surprise. I would be happy to exercise with such a beautiful woman."

I asked her about the kids and she explained that the neighbor was watching them along with her own kids. They were doing their homework together.

Since the square was on the way home we both drove our cars there and parked. She asked me about what stretches she needed to do. I think she already knew. She just enjoyed making me feel needed and important. She had always kept herself in good shape and knew how to jog, and she looked great doing so! After a few stretches, off we went.

My run started off a little different than normal. My wife tried to carry on a meaningful conversation while we were running, but quickly realized it made you very winded, very quickly. After a minor break to catch her breath, she was back to her normal running pace. I was glad, too, because I used my jogging to relax and unwind. Trying to talk while I was running wasn't going to work for me at all. After a few minutes we were able to keep a good pace without talking. You don't have to talk to enjoy someone's company. I didn't think it would work at first but came to understand that I really did enjoy her there with me.

Normally my wife did her walking and running on our treadmill inside with the air conditioner. Running outside in the sun and heat was new to her, and it was starting to show. I noticed that sweat was starting to bead up on the top of her lip and forehead. She also was wearing a complete jogging suit while I usually ran in shorts and a T-shirt. I could tell she hadn't taken the heat into consideration.

She turned and looked at me and saw a look on my face that she hadn't seen in a while. It was a look of concern. At that point our pace had slowed down a bit because we were a little winded. We finally slowed to a walk. She asked:

"What's wrong?"

"Nothing," I said. "I don't want you to over do it. You look exhausted."

"Yeah, I'm really tired. But I can still out run your rear end! We'll see who gets to the square first."

With that challenge in place she took off running as I chased behind her. She made it to the square first. I let her win, although she will tell you differently. I stopped and watched as Elizabeth ran around the square one more time with her hands raised in victory and a big smile on her face. I had never seen her look so beautiful. I let her enjoy her time of glory. I knew I would gain a lot of brownie points for allowing that to happen.

My wife went and sat down on one of the benches while I took my new sweat towel and wet it with the water from the fountain. I took it to her first so she could refresh herself by wiping her face. Then I went and wet the towel a second time for myself. As I returned to my wife, she was looking off to the other side of the square behind me. She nodded her head and asked, "What's wrong with that guy?" I turned to look and saw a nicely dressed gentleman standing off to the side by himself. He was literally just standing there with his hands covering his face.

"I don't know. It is only one of a few strange things that have happened over the last few days. I suppose it could be anything." My eyes automatically started scanning across the square.

"What are you looking for?" my wife asked.

"I'm looking for the Bag Man. He usually shows up right about now."

"Is that him over there?" My wife pointed in the opposite direction from where I was looking.

"Yes, that's him all right."

"Huh, he looks a lot older than you described him. I thought he would be younger."

"Yeah, he seems to have aged a lot over the last few days. Weird."

I sat down next to my wife, and we both watched as the Bag Man made his way over to the guy that had his hands over his face. The Bag Man finally approached the guy, standing face-to-face with him. He said something to the guy, but once again I was too far away to hear what he said. Still with his hands covering his face, the guy shook his head no in a very persistent manner. The guy leaned back against the side of the building and lowered himself down to a seated position. The Bag Man lowered his bag from his shoulder and sat it down on the ground next to the guy. He opened his bag and reached into it and pulled out what looked like a small blanket of some kind. He opened up the blanket and draped it over the guy, including his head, leaving only a small portion of his face showing, enough that he could see him as he talked to him. We were too far away to see who it was, though.

My wife turned to me and said, "Why did he do that?"

I replied, "I don't know, honey. We just have to wait and see."

The Bag Man moved himself to a kneeling position in front of the guy and began to talk to him. I could tell by the body language of the gentleman that he was crying from deep down in his soul. Whatever was bothering him really affected him emotionally. Even though we couldn't hear what the Bag Man was saying, we could hear the gentleman crying deeply. I don't think my wife had ever seen a man cry like that before. When I glanced at her I could see tears forming in the corners of her eyes. It was starting to affect her in an emotional way.

Still with her eyes fixed on the two men, she muttered these words, "Should we go over and help?"

"No" I said. "He will let us know if he needs our help."

After a few minutes the gentleman's crying subsided. My wife took my sweat towel and wiped her face again, eliminating the tears from her eyes. Both the gentleman and the Bag Man remained silent for a few seconds. Finally the gentleman, still with the blanket covering his head, nodded his head yes. The

Bag Man started talking again. A couple of minutes later, the Bag Man stood up and pulled the blanket off of the gentleman. He folded the blanket and put it back in his bag. The gentleman stood up and shook the Bag Man's hand. They both walked away in different directions. The Bag Man never once made eye contact with us. My wife looked me in the eyes and said, "I now understand what you meant when you said it was frustrating not knowing what happened." We walked to our cars and left.

When we entered the door of our house my wife said, "The neighbors called me on the way home and said the kids could stay the night at their house." After we hit the showers we were able to just sit and enjoy each other's company without the kids. After relaxing for a little while we headed off to bed. We were so exhausted we just laid there in each others arms.

My wife spoke first, "I wonder what actually happened on the square tonight."

"I can only imagine at this point." I said.

"How do you deal with that feeling?"

"Knowing that one day, at the right time, it will reveal itself to you."

"That's hard."

"Trust me, I know."

With those words, we fell asleep in each other's arms.

day

TWELVE

It was Friday morning, and I woke to the normal smell of breakfast cooking. After a quick shower and getting dressed for work, I went downstairs to the kitchen. My wife was at the sink washing the dishes. I snuck up behind her and put my arms around her waist. Knowing it was me, she leaned her head back onto my shoulder. I brushed her long, flowing, brown hair out of the way with my hand. I leaned down and kissed the side of her neck.

We fixed our plates and sat down at the table to eat together. My wife started the conversation.

"What would you say if I told you that we had all weekend without the kids?"

"I would say wonderful!"

"Good. The neighbor called and wanted the kids to stay all weekend for a birthday party at their pool. I said yes. So we are kid-less till Sunday night."

"Would you like for me to make reservations for dinner tonight?" I said.

"No, I've got a ladies banquet at church tonight. I won't be home from there till about ten-ish. Just grab you something to eat tonight, and we'll go out tomorrow night instead."

"Okay, I'll make that happen."

"By the way, I won't be able to go jogging with you after work today. As much as I enjoyed it yesterday, I have to be at church early to help set things up for the banquet and clean up afterwards. So you are on your own till I get home."

We kissed, and off to work I went.

It was a typical day at work, filled with decisions and stress. I was glad it was Friday and glad I was off for the weekend. When I left work I went directly to the square and parked in the usual spot. I was looking forward to my run for the day. I needed to release my work stress so I could enjoy my weekend with my wife. While I was running I was so focused on planning the weekend with my wife, without the kids, that I didn't even think about the Bag Man. Not even once. Normally I would at least have him in the back of my mind, but not today.

I decided to run a little longer time and distance since I was by myself and nobody was at home waiting on me. So I was running later than normal. There was no need for me to be in a hurry, so I just took my time.

I was on my way back to the square when I heard a gut-wrenching scream from one of the side streets across from the other side of the square. I turned my attention in that direction to see where it came from. What I saw was a woman struggling with a man. He was wearing a black hooded sweatshirt with the hood pulled over his head. He was pulling on the woman's purse trying to steal it from her. She was holding on to the straps, trying to keep him from getting it. She screamed for help once again. That made the man even more determined. He put his hand in his pocket and pulled something out. From a distance it looked like a knife. I realized what was about to happen and reacted by yelling with all my strength, "*Hey, stop!*"

He hesitated and looked at me. "*Don't do it!*" I yelled.

Before I could even get those words out of my mouth he had plunged the knife into the woman's chest. Falling to the ground, the woman let go of her purse. The man ran away with the purse in his hands as I ran to help the woman.

Another man got there a little sooner than I did. When I got there the other guy had all ready turned the body over. He put his fingers to the woman's throat to see if she had a pulse. She was barely alive. I assumed that he was a doctor or someone who had medical training. I could see the knife sticking out of her chest as she lay on her back. I had my sweat towel in my pocket so I got it out. I tried to put it around the wound but the other man pushed it away. I got out my cell phone and called 911. As I was explaining what happened, the other man reached up and grabbed the knife that was sticking out of the woman's chest. He was trying to pull it out.

I grabbed the man's hands and tried to stop him, yelling, "Don't pull it out. She'll bleed to death before help can get here!" He grabbed me and quickly shoved me away, leaving bloodstains on my shirt. He turned his head and looked into my eyes. It was then that I realized who the other man was. It was the Bag Man.

I backed up and stayed out of his way. I hoped that maybe he knew something that I didn't know. I was on the phone with the 911 operator. I thought that was my way of helping. Before I could stop him, the Bag Man grabbed the handle of the knife, and in one swift move pulled it out of her chest. He dropped the knife as blood started gushing out of the wound. He lifted his head and looked down the street as he heard the sirens from the ambulance as it got closer. He had a look of desperation on his face. He suddenly pulled his shirt open and quickly took it off. He wadded it up and placed it on top of the wound and put pressure on it. It looked like he was trying to stop the bleeding.

He lifted his head again to look for the ambulance. I thought he was going to explain to the paramedics what had happened. But that is not what he did. What he did next was something I didn't understand. He removed his shirt from the woman's wound and put it back on as if he was going to wear it. As the ambulance came into view, I could see a police car coming from the other direction. The Bag Man stood up and ran down the alley, leaving the woman there alone. He was acting like he didn't want anyone to see him there. At that point a crowd had started to gather around to see what the commotion was about.

The police car pulled up first and Officer Smith and another officer got out of the car. They quickly assessed the scene and directed the ambulance where to come. While the police and paramedics were taking care of the woman with the stab wound, I walked down the alley to see if I could find the Bag Man.

I was at the other end of the alley when I saw him. He was sitting down next to a dumpster, and was leaning against a wall. From the street light I could see that he was breathing very hard. When I reached him I asked him why he ran away. That's when I realized the seriousness on his face. He looked like he was in pain and had his hand pressed against his chest. His shirt was soaked in blood. I assumed it was the woman's blood because of the amount on his shirt. It was only after I knelt down next to him that I knew I was wrong. I could see more blood coming from under his hand. I moved his hand out of the way and opened his shirt, revealing the source of the blood. He had a large wound on his chest and blood was gushing profusely from it.

I quickly turned toward the ambulance and screamed at the top of my lungs, *"Help! I need help here!"*

As I turned facing him again, he grabbed my shirt and pulled himself closer to me. He was trying to say something. As I leaned closer to hear him, he looked me in the eyes with that soul-searching stare, and he whispered in a low voice, "You finish what I started!"

Still looking into my eyes, he gasped for air. He let go of my shirt and closed his eyes and fell back against the wall. His body was limp. I knew he had taken his last breath, and died.

Not knowing what was going on, Officer Smith came running down the alley with her gun drawn and pointed upwards. She had no idea what she was about to walk into. Following close behind her was a paramedic. Once the scene was secure, the paramedic started working on the Bag Man. I knew that he wouldn't be able to help him; he was already dead. I was standing out of the way up against a wall watching them. I couldn't believe what was happening. Maybe I didn't want to.

The paramedic turned and looked at the officer and shook his head no. Officer Smith looked at me and then walked over to me. She got out her notepad and pen.

"Did you see what happened to him or the woman?"

"Yes, I saw what happened to both of them."

"Do you know who they are?"

"I don't know the woman. I've seen him around town a few times, but I don't really know him or his name. I call him 'the Bag Man.'"

"Tell me what happened."

I started telling her what happened, beginning at the time I arrived at the square that night. It was a difficult story to tell. It was a difficult story for the officer to believe. I had to tell her the story several times to get her to understand. Finally, I told her everything that I had witnessed over the last couple of weeks. There was an awkward moment of silence at the end of my story. Then she broke the silence.

"There have been rumors of a guy doing weird things over the last couple of weeks. You're telling me that he is that guy?"

"Yes. If I hadn't seen it with my own eyes I wouldn't have believed it myself."

When I finished that statement, the other officer and the other paramedic walked up to us and began talking. The paramedic spoke first.

"All of the witnesses agree and said that the woman was stabbed, and that the other victim tried to help her. But I can't find a single wound of any kind on the woman's chest. There is blood everywhere, there is a knife, but no knife wound. The story they are telling just doesn't make any sense. We will take her to the hospital to have her checked out, but I think she will be fine. She doesn't remember much right now. We will drop him off at the county morgue. Call me if you find any more information."

The paramedics put the Bag Man on the gurney and pushed him past me toward the ambulance. I felt sadness and a great loss. He only helped other people. He didn't deserve to die. Officer Smith gave me her business card and told me to call her if I thought of anything else that might be helpful.

———

When I arrived back home, my wife hadn't gotten home from church, and the house was empty. I was drained and lay down on the couch in the den. I couldn't keep from going over and over in my head what had happened. I had my eyes closed and was so focused on the situation that I didn't hear when my wife came in the door. When she turned the lights on she saw me lying on my back covered in blood, and my eyes were closed. She immediately went into panic mode. She screamed, *"Oh my god!"*

She ran over to the couch and fell to her knees. She grabbed my arms and started shaking me, calling my name. It startled me because I didn't hear her come in. I opened my eyes but was in a daze. She ripped my shirt open.

"Where are you hurt?"

"What?"

"Where are you hurt? You're bleeding."

"What are you talking about?"

"You're bleeding. Where is the blood coming from? Where are you hurt?"

"I'm not hurt. It's not my blood."

"What?"

"It's not my blood!"

When I said that her emotions changed, and in one swift motion she slapped me across my face. I had no idea what was going on. She jumped and put her arms around my neck and squeezed me tightly and started to cry. When I finally got her calmed down enough to talk, she said, "Don't you ever scare me like that again!"

It wasn't until then that I looked down and noticed my appearance. I didn't realize that my shirt was covered in blood. That, along with me lying on my back with my eyes closed, must have made me look like I was dead.

"I'm sorry. I didn't mean to scare you."

"If it's not your blood, then whose blood is it?"

I stood up and walked across the room as my wife sat on the edge of the couch.

"I said whose blood is it?"

"It's the Bag Man's blood."

"What happened?"

I turned and walked back over to the couch and sat down next to her. She took my hand in hers and said, "Tell me what happened."

I told her everything that happened that night. I told her about the woman, the knife, the stabbing, the police, and the death of the Bag Man. I left nothing out. Tears were flowing down my face as I told her the story. I emptied myself of all sorrow, all pain, and all guilt. She leaned back and pulled my head to her bosom. She held me there tightly as I emptied myself of all emotion. With my head on her chest, I wept bitterly, and she wept along with me. It must have been at least fifteen minutes before I was able to regain control of my emotions. My wife had never seen me weep like that, and never has seen me that vulnerable before. I was a broken man. She wasn't about to leave my side, and I'm glad she didn't! I couldn't have made it through those emotions without her strength and her stability.

We didn't sleep much that night. We mainly talked about the Bag Man and how we wish we had known him better. Normally we lay in bed while I held my wife in my arms until she fell asleep. That night it was opposite. She held me in her arms all night long.

If she slept any at all, it was during the few times I dozed off briefly. Every time I opened my eyes she was watching me, taking care of me. I couldn't ask for a better soul mate.

day

THIRTEEN

It was early morning, about 6:00 a.m., when I turned over and noticed that my wife had fallen asleep. She was so exhausted from taking care of me all night. I eased my way out of bed so as not to wake her. I quietly got dressed. I couldn't sleep so I decided to go to the square and walk around and examine my thoughts. I left a note for my wife so she wouldn't be worried about me. I just needed some alone time to work things out in my head.

I knew that walking the square would not be an easy thing to do, considering what happened the night before. I just needed to face the facts straightforward to get beyond them. It proved to be more difficult than I had imagined it would be. For the last two weeks I had always run into the Bag Man somewhere close to the square, but not that day. That day would be different, and it somehow made me feel all alone.

It was Saturday about 6:30 a.m., and the traffic was almost nonexistent. Most people were off from work and still in bed. I saw an occasional car pass by, but nothing to really speak of. There was one vehicle that pulled up to the curb on the other side of the street where I was standing. It was the newspaper delivery guy. He opened the newspaper box and took the old papers out, and replaced them with new papers, and then drove away. I walked across the street to look and see what the headlines of the paper read. To my surprise, the headline read: "Unknown man killed last night during altercation on the square." I bought one of the papers from the box and read the story. It made me angry because they left out several vital parts of the story. They didn't even mention the woman at all. The only bit of information that was of any use to me was it mentioned that the John Doe would be buried in the county cemetery on Sunday and a short grave-side service would be conducted. It didn't mention a time of day or anything. Disappointed, I folded the newspaper and put it under my arm and then walked away.

Before I knew it I was back at the location where it all happened the night before. A portion of the street and the whole alley was blocked off with yellow crime scene tape. I just stood there and stared down the alley, replaying the whole thing over and over in my head. After a few minutes I went under the crime scene tape and walked down the alley. I knew it was wrong, but I couldn't help myself. I felt compelled to do so. When I reached the other end of the alley, where the Bag Man died, I knelt down next to the dried pool of blood on the ground. Once again I became emotional and started to cry. I had to get it out of my system, so I uttered these words, "I'm sorry I let you die. I should have done more to save you." Once I said those words I felt better, but it still didn't change the fact that he was dead.

After a brief moment of silence, I stood up to walk away. That's when I saw something out of the corner of my eye that caught my attention. It was behind the dumpster. When I leaned down to get a closer look, I realized what it was. It was the Bag Man's duffel bag. He must have hidden it back there last night before I found him. Apparently the police didn't see it last night either. I pulled the bag from behind the dumpster. I looked around, and no one was in sight. I walked back to the entrance of the alley, still no one in sight. I didn't know what to do, so I carried the bag to my car and drove home with it.

When I arrived home, I went directly to the living room and sat down on the couch. The house was quiet so I leaned my head back and closed my eyes. I wasn't sleepy, but I was emotionally exhausted. A few minutes later, Elizabeth entered the living room where I was sitting. She had a cup of coffee in each hand, one for me and one for her. She gave me one and then sat down on the couch next to me. She saw the duffel bag on the coffee table and said, "What's that?"

"It's a duffel bag."

"I can see that. Whose duffel bag is it?"

"The Bag Man's."

"Where did you get it?"

"I found it."

"Are we going to play twenty questions here, or are you going to tell me about this bag?"

"Okay. I went for a walk on the square this morning to clear my head. I found myself in the alley where the Bag Man died. Before I left I found his duffel bag behind the dumpster he was sitting next to. I picked it up and brought it home with me."

"Did you open it and look inside?"

"No."

"Well, will you?"

"Yes, but not right now."

"When?"

"Later."

"Have you called the police yet to let them know you found it?"

"No."

"Are you going to?"

"Yes."

"Here we go with the twenty questions again."

"I will call them when I get ready to. It has no bearing on the case anyway."

"How do you know?"

"I just know."

"Okay, but don't get yourself in trouble with the police."

After sitting there quietly for a few minutes, I reached over and picked up the newspaper and gave it to my wife and asked her to read the article on the front page. After reading the article she was a little upset.

"They left out part of the story."

"I know."

"Well that's wrong."

"I know."

"Why don't you call the paper and give them the whole story?"

"What good would it do?"

"At least you will be honoring the Bag Man. Don't you think everyone needs to know the real story about him?"

"Maybe you're right. I'll call them later."

After a brief moment of silence Elizabeth continued.

"Do you want to go to the graveside service?"

"I would like to."

"I'll call around today and see if I can find out what time the service is."

"Thank you."

We both got up and took a shower and got dressed. We decided to go out for breakfast instead of my wife cooking. Afterwards we went shopping and bought a few things for the house. I know what my wife was trying to do. She was trying to get me out of the house and keep me busy so that I wouldn't get so depressed about the situation with the Bag Man. It helped some, but still, it was in the back of my head all day. When we got home I lay on the bed and turned on the television to see what I could find that was interesting. My wife started making a few phone calls to find out about the graveside service. When she finished she came upstairs and lay on the bed next to me. We both fell asleep watching TV. That was all we did for the rest of the day.

day

FOURTEEN

PART ONE

When I woke the next morning I was very uneasy. I didn't get much sleep and felt like a part of my life was coming to an end. We got up and ate breakfast as usual. It was quieter than normal because the kids were still spending the weekend at the neighbor's house, and neither of us was engaging in conversation very well. My wife finally broke the silence.

"I found out the funeral for the Bag Man is at noon at the county cemetery. I assume you still want to go?"

"Yes, I do want to go."

"I don't want you to be disappointed, but you do realize that we will probably be the only ones there, except for the cemetery workers and the preacher conducting the service? After all, nobody really knows who he is or even his real name."

"I know, but I feel like I need to be there for him. I owe him at least that much. Besides, it's the right thing to do."

"I was just making sure you still wanted to go. You get in the shower first, and I'll clean up the dishes while you're in there."

I got up and headed for the shower. I was still a little tired from not sleeping well, so a hot shower was exactly what I needed to get me going. At some point in everyone's life, no matter how much you love your spouse there comes times when you just need to be by yourself. My shower time was usually my alone time. It's time alone to think and work stuff out without people seeing me or hearing me. That's why I took so long in the shower; it's my only time alone. The hot water beating down on my head and shoulders, and the steam it created, helped me to relax. While in the shower I did something that I haven't done in quite a while. I talked to God. That didn't mean that I hadn't prayed in a while, I did that pretty regular. I mean I really talked to him and took time for him to talk back. I couldn't get over the fact that the Bag Man, a good guy, had to die. I needed answers. The only answer I got was an overwhelming feeling that I would find out soon enough. My time alone ended when my wife came in and said she needed to take a shower also. In other words, hurry up and get out!

When we pulled into the parking lot at the cemetery I noticed a few cars there but not many. I thought they were the cars of the workers of the cemetery. When we walked down the sidewalk leading to the gravesites, my wife held on to my arm and wouldn't let go of it. I didn't know if she was just nervous or was concerned about me. She wasn't going to leave my side. We made it down to the gravesite and just stood there alone. We weren't even sure it was the right one or not. Soon afterwards a man in nice clothes came up and stood at the head of the coffin. I assumed that he was the preacher in charge. He spoke and shook our hands, and introduced himself as such.

After a couple of minutes, a few people started to gather around. First it was one at a time, then by twos and threes. The preacher would greet them as they came up. Most people were dressed in casual clothing and some were dressed in very nice clothes. Finally, one last person arrived and stood at the foot of the coffin. It was Officer Smith. I almost didn't recognize her because she wasn't wearing her police uniform. I made eye contact with her and nodded. She returned the gesture. I guess in all there were about twenty to twenty-five people that gathered together around the gravesite.

The minister in charge spoke with authority and grace. He was very kind with his words and spoke as if he had known the Bag Man for some time. I had only known him about two weeks, and I didn't know much about him. I don't remember much of what the preacher said; it was all kind of fuzzy in my head.

As I glanced around at the people that gathered; they were all focused on the preacher. Why was my mind different and unable to focus? That's when I recognized one of them. When I did I almost gasped for air. My wife leaned in and asked if I was all right. I nodded yes. There, standing next to a man and woman, was the little deaf boy that I almost hit with my car the week before. I reasoned that the man and woman must be his parents. The boy was actually in tears. As I continued to look around the small crowd of people, I noticed someone else who looked familiar. She stood out in the crowd. It was that very nice looking blonde woman. I recognized her because of the style of clothing she was wearing. She was in tears also.

Several of the people there were people I had seen over the last two weeks because of the Bag Man. Several of the people I didn't recognize. But I had this strange feeling that they were connected to the Bag Man.

I could tell by the tone that the preacher had in his voice that the short service was about to come to an end. Finally he prayed a simple prayer. It wasn't one of eloquent or large words you would normally hear from most people who pray out loud. But it was more powerful than any other prayer I've heard any other preacher pray. After the prayer, everyone stepped to the side as the workers began to lower the casket into the ground. It was so reverent and quiet that you could hear a pin drop. As the casket hit the bottom of the grave, one of the ladies began to sing. It was a familiar song, and we all joined in and sang with her, "I am the Bag Man, the Bag Man I am he, come see the Bag Man, and see what you can be." My wife stood and watched with pleasure as we all sang in unison the song that would permanently be etched in our minds.

When the song ended everyone just stood there, waiting to see what was going to happen next. I always carried business cards in my pocket. I felt inspired that something more should be done for the Bag Man, so I walked around, weaving throughout the small amount of people that were gathered there. I gave each person one of my business cards and told them that I was having a gathering at my house later that evening and wanted them to come and be a part of it. Most people didn't say anything, they just nodded as they walked away. I also gave one of my cards to Officer Smith and told her that I had something at my house that belonged to the Bag Man that she needed to know about. Then I told her about the gathering at my house that evening. She said that she would be there to look at it then.

The people that were there at the gravesite had walked away, a few at a time, until me and my wife were the only two left standing there.

"Are you all right?" Elizabeth asked as she placed her hand on my shoulder.

"I will be," I responded.

I turned and faced her. Pulling her hand from my shoulder and taking both of her hands in mine, I looked directly into her eyes and said, "I'm sorry for putting you on the spot like this but I decided to have some people from the funeral over to the house tonight. I invited everyone."

"Oh," she said. "Why?"

"I just feel like it's something I have to do."

She pulled her hands from mine and placed her arms around my neck giving me a slight hug and a soft kiss on the cheek. She whispered into my ear, "It's okay. I forgive you. We're in this thing together."

While we were driving down the road, my wife informed me that we needed to pick up a few things for the gathering and discussed what I had in mind for it. We decided to make it simple and have only a few snacks and finger foods along with something to drink.

When we arrived home my wife told me to lie down. I was so exhausted even though we hadn't really done anything. I guess my mind was so confused and tired that my body was also. She started getting things together as I fell across the bed. I kicked my shoes off and fell asleep almost instantly. I don't think I could have made it through the day without some extra rest.

day

FOURTEEN

PART TWO

The next thing I remember was my wife waking me from my sleep. It was about 6:30 p.m., which gave me about thirty minutes to freshen up before everyone was supposed to show up. Both of us washed our faces and changed clothes to feel more comfortable. We were as ready as we were going to be. I really had no idea how many people were actually going to show up. And I didn't even know what I was going to say or do. All I knew was that I needed to do this. I was compelled to do this, whatever this was.

As it happened at the gravesite, it happened again. People started showing up sporadically, a few at a time here and there. We offered drinks and snacks to each of them. After a few minutes, everyone that was at the gravesite was now in my living room, except Officer Smith. The preacher had other commitments. There were even a few extra people there that didn't attend the funeral earlier. As with any gathering, people were talking and getting to know one another. They talked about the general stuff like work and home life. Some people were so quiet that we still didn't know anything more about them than their names. Nobody seemed to mention anything about the Bag Man or how they knew him. Maybe they just didn't know what to say, or how to say it. Some of the people were very open and outgoing, while others were very quiet and only talked if you asked them questions. Even then they gave very vague answers.

After we spent a few minutes of mingling together, Officer Smith finally showed up. She had some issues that needed to be taken care of before she came and was running a little late. After she got there I had everyone gather in the large living room and asked them to have a seat.

My wife pulled me aside and kissed me on the cheek and asked, "What are you going to say?"

"I don't know. I'm playing this one by ear. But when the time comes, God will give me the words to say."

"I don't think I've ever seen this leader side of you so bold before. I'm impressed."

"Stand by my side?"

"As always."

I felt her support as she gently squeezed my hand. I needed it too, because I was nervous. I had spoken in front of small crowds before, but only at work and about work-related things. I had never spoken to a group of people about death and life matters. I wondered if I had what it took to do so.

As I stood before them at the edge of the room, all eyes were upon me. Some eyes were cold and mysterious, while others were happy and inviting. Still, some were cautious-looking eyes. I took a deep breath before I began to speak. As I opened my mouth, I hesitated. An encouraging look from my wife got me going again.

I introduced my wife and myself, and we thanked them for coming by. I told them about my experience with the Bag Man and how it had affected me. I fumbled my words a little, but I managed to get my story told. No one said a word as I spoke. It made me wonder if I was doing the right thing. But my spirit said I needed to continue. I didn't go into detail about every good thing that I saw the Bag Man do, I just said I saw him do many good things for people. Quite honestly, in some cases I really had no idea what he did. Only what I physically saw.

As I finished speaking I wondered how the people were going to react. Unfortunately, no one said anything. There was a moment of awkward silence. I didn't know why, but what I did know was that I needed to do this in order for me to move beyond this feeling I had inside of me. I was determined to continue.

I walked over to the other side of the room to a table that my wife and I had set earlier that evening. The table had the duffel bag on it, but it was covered with a table cloth. I looked in the direction of Officer Smith and started speaking again.

"Officer Smith, I would like for you to come up front and take a look at something for me."

Officer Smith graciously walked up to the table. I pulled the table cloth from the table revealing the duffel bag for everyone to see. Immediately several people in the group gasped as they recognized it was the Bag Man's duffel bag that he carried around with him. I could tell that some people, as well as Officer Smith, didn't know what it was. So I explained it.

"As you can see this is a duffel bag, but not just any duffel bag. It's the Bag Man's duffel bag. He carried it with him everywhere he went."

I explained to Officer Smith and everyone in the crowd how I ended up with possession of the bag.

"I invited all of you here tonight because I wanted you to see it. I haven't opened it yet and have no idea what is inside of it. I felt it would be nice for all of us to see what's inside together as a group."

Again I focused on Officer Smith.

"Because you are an officer of the law, I would like for you to open the bag and see what's inside."

"I would be honored to do so," she said. "But let me go to my car and get a pair of gloves. Safety first you know."

When Officer Smith came back inside she opened the bag. She shuffled things around inside the bag at first without pulling anything out. She said, "There doesn't appear to be anything dangerous inside the bag. It looks like it only has some old personal items of no value inside."

When she was satisfied that there was nothing dangerous or illegal in the bag, she began to take the items out of the bag one at a time. The people were standing and sitting very still, and they were extremely quiet. You could literally hear a pin drop. Their eyes were fixed on Officer Smith with anticipation of what she was going to pull out of the bag.

The first item she pulled out of the bag was an old, dusty pair of earmuffs. Everyone had a look of puzzlement on their faces, trying to figure out why the Bag Man carried around earmuffs. Suddenly from the corner of the room a woman put her hand to her mouth and gasped with excitement. The man standing next to her put his arm around her and pulled her close. Both of them had tears in their eyes. The boy that was standing in front of them stepped out and came to the front of the room and stood facing Officer Smith. He put his hand out and pointed at the earmuffs. Smith asked him if he wanted the earmuffs, and the boy shook his head yes. She gave him the earmuffs and the boy walked back and stood by his parents.

I had an overwhelming feeling that there was a story behind the earmuffs, so I spoke up.

"Ma'am, tell us about the earmuffs, please."

At first she struggled to speak through her tears, but then she regained control of her emotions.

"My name is Jennifer Glass, and this is my husband, Mike. This is our twelve-year-old son, Chad. When Chad was only five years old, he had a severe ear infection in both ears. It was a recurring problem that we were having difficulty controlling. After a while we were able to get rid of it, but the damage had already been done. The severe infections left him deaf in both ears. Not even surgery could help him to hear. We sent him to private schools for the deaf and they were able to teach him to use sign language. He got pretty good at it, and for seven years that has been his main way of communication, except for writing notes."

While the woman was still speaking the boy reached up and tugged on his mother's dress. She stopped talking long enough to see what he wanted. He talked to her using sign language. She shook her head yes. She looked back at us with a smile on her face and said, "He wants to tell the rest of the story. Chad still has to re-learn how to speak correctly, so he will use sign language and his father will translate it for you."

The father moved to the side so he could see the boy's hands. As the boy began to sign, the father began to speak.

"A few months ago I wasn't doing so well. I wasn't sick or anything like that, but I was sad a lot and didn't want to go to school anymore. I didn't have many real good friends except for a couple of other deaf kids. Nobody really wants to be friends with a deaf person unless they are deaf, too. Mom and dad decided to make me go off to different places with them so I wouldn't be depressed so much. I don't really know what that means, but I think they didn't want me to be sad all the time. One day we went to the square where the big fountain is. They wanted to go in the stores and look around. I didn't want to do that so they let me hang out around the fountain as long as I didn't go anywhere else without letting them know first. While I was outside looking at the fountain, a man came and sat down on the bench next to me. He started talking to me using sign language. I don't know how he knew I was deaf because I had never seen him before, but somehow he knew. Dad always told me not to talk to strangers, but for some reason I knew this guy was different.

"We started talking in sign language. I told him my name, and he told me to call him by his nickname, 'Bag Man.' I think that's because he always carried a big bag around with him. After talking with him I always felt better about things so I started walking up to the square as much as I could. It didn't matter what day or what time it was, he was always there to talk to me. My parents didn't know where I was, they thought I was always outside playing or hiding out in my tree house that dad built for me. I spend a lot of time there. I know it was wrong to do that but sometimes I just needed a friend to talk to. He became my best friend, and I could talk to him about anything. He understood how I felt.

"A few days ago I was on my way to the square to see the Bag Man because I was really upset about something. I wasn't really paying attention to where I was walking because I was in a hurry to get to the Bag Man. As I was crossing the street I looked up and saw a car coming toward me. I was in the middle of the road, and a car was about to hit me. I just froze and didn't know what to do. The car slammed on his breaks, and I fell to the ground. It felt like somebody pushed me down instead of the car hitting me. All I know for sure is that I was scared!

"When everything stopped moving, a man got out of the car and ran around to check on me, to make sure I was all right." The boy pointed at me and said, "I think you are the man." I nodded my head yes. "I was curled up in a ball lying on the ground. I was crying so much that I couldn't talk. You didn't know at the time that I was deaf and couldn't hear you talking to me. I was so scared that all I could think to do was to get up and run away, run to my friend the Bag Man.

"When I found him he could tell that something was wrong by the way I was acting. He asked me what happened, and I told him everything. I also told him I was tired of being made fun of and treated differently because I couldn't hear. I told him I was tired of not being normal or at least feeling normal. I wanted to be a normal, everyday kid. I didn't want to be deaf anymore. I wanted to hear again!

"We talked for a little while longer, and then he told me that he could help me hear again. I asked him how, but he didn't answer my question. He simply said that it was important that I believe that he could help me, and that I must be sure that I wanted it more than anything else. I nodded my head yes. He reached down and picked up his bag and put it in his lap. He opened the bag and pulled out this pair of earmuffs. After moving his bag out of the way he looked me in the eyes and asked me again if I wanted him to help me hear. I nodded my head yes one more time.

"The Bag Man closed his eyes and slightly bowed his head and started talking. I thought he was talking to me at first, but then I realized that he was praying. I could see his lips move but didn't know what he was saying because I can't read lips yet. After he finished praying he opened his eyes and looked at me with a big smile on his face. It was like he was about to get a birthday present or Christmas gift, or something like that. He seemed excited! He opened up the earmuffs and put them on my head and adjusted them over my ears. With sign language he asked me if I heard anything. With a sad look on my face I shook my head no. He signed again saying that it was okay, all I needed to do was believe, close my eyes, and listen.

"I did what he told me to do. At first I heard nothing. Then I heard some very faint noises. I opened my eyes and looked at the Bag Man. I think that smile on his face got even bigger! I closed my eyes again and started concentrating on the noise I was hearing. The noise gradually got louder and clearer. I realized it was music of some kind. Then without warning I heard people singing words with the music. It was the most beautiful sound imaginable. It was so wonderful that I felt it all over my body as it surrounded me. It was so powerful that I began to shake. Those were the first words I've heard in seven years. These were the words I heard: 'Holy, Holy, Holy, is the Lord Jesus.' The music and the words just repeated over and over again. I will never forget them as long as I live!

"I turned and looked at the Bag Man. I could see tears as they started rolling down his face, tears of joy. He reached up and pulled the earmuffs from my head and put them back into his bag. He looked back at me and said, 'Can you hear me now?' I tried to answer him by speaking, but it just didn't sound right, so I nodded my head yes. He told me that I would have to re-learn how to speak, but I could hear just fine. He told me to go home and tell my parents about what happened and show them that I can now hear again. As I turned and started walking away I could hear what was going on around me. I was excited about hearing again, but at the same time I was kind of scared too, because it was new to me. I turned and saw the Bag Man still watching me. I walked back to where he was. He asked me what was wrong. In sign language, I told him nothing was wrong. I just wanted to say thank you for helping me hear. And, thank you for being my friend.

"As I walked home my new life began. I told my parents what happened. We went to the doctors, and they were amazed that I could hear. They couldn't explain how. We went back to the square several times to talk to the Bag Man, but we couldn't find him. Now we know why. He was my best friend, and I will miss him a lot."

The boy walked back over to his parents and stood by them as a family should. After a few seconds of silence Officer Smith began to shuffle things around in the bag again. Everyone's attention once again shifted toward her.

The second item that Officer Smith pulled out of the bag was an old, dusty, wrinkled up baseball cap. An older man walked up and asked for the hat. As Smith gave it to him, he turned to face the crowd and began to speak with a humble spirit.

"My name is Charles Avery, and I am fifty-nine years old."

As he pointed in the direction of the younger couple with him, he said, "And this young man is my son and his wife, John and Margaret Avery. When I was a young man of eighteen years old I married the most beautiful woman in the world. As we started our life together we were full of life and excitement. A year later she became pregnant, and nine months later John was born. Several years later all of the stresses of life began to wear on me very heavy. In a moment of weakness, on a business trip, I fell into temptation and was unfaithful to my wife. We divorced shortly afterwards. I left the family and never spoke to her or my son again. The only contact I made with my son was an occasional birthday card in the mail and a monthly child support check. She eventually got married again to a very nice man who took care of her and raised my son.

"Two years ago I heard that she had cancer and wasn't doing well. She tracked me down, somehow, using the Internet. When she found me she asked me to come and see her. I followed the directions that she gave me and found her at home. When she invited me in I sat there quietly, not knowing what to say. Finally

I got up and walked over toward where she was sitting and fell to my knees. I was so overwhelmed by my guilt that I just broke down and started crying my eyes out. Over and over, I begged her to forgive me for what I had done to her and John."

As I looked over at John and Margaret, I noticed that both of them were weeping openly. I walked over to give them some tissues. It was apparent to me that this was the first time they had heard this story. After the short interruption Charles continued to speak.

"As I continued to beg for forgiveness some thirty-nine years later, she gently lifted my face and wiped the tears from my eyes with a tissue. With her sitting on the edge of her chair, and me on my knees in front of her, she cradled my face with both hands and said, 'Charles, I forgave you a long time ago. It wasn't easy, but I did it with God's help. John, on the other hand, is still angry and bitter toward even the mention of your name.' I got up off of the floor and sat in the chair across from her. After regaining my composure, we sat and talked for hours. I was glad that she was happy and found love again with a good man. Neither of us spoke of this meeting until now. She said I would know when to tell it. Now is that time.

"She asked nothing from me except one favor: Somehow, some way, make it right with John. I promised her that I would. When I left there that day I never saw nor spoke to her again. Four months later, I heard that she passed away from cancer. From that point forward I knew what I had to do concerning John, but that proved to be more difficult than I had ever thought possible. I had hurt him a lot, and his bitterness and hatred for me ran very deep in his heart.

"The only time I ever met this Bag Man that everyone keeps talking about was a couple of weeks ago on the square. I will never forget that day. Officer Smith, you were there responding to a disorderly conduct scene on the square."

She nodded her head in agreement.

"That was us. I had tried several times talking to my son, but he wouldn't have anything to do with me. I actually saw him and his wife there by accident. I figured that since he was with his wife he would be more reasonable and open to speaking with me. Boy, was I wrong! It only made things worse because I now involved his wife, who didn't even know I existed. Still, she was the only reasonable one of the three of us. As it turned ugly between John and me in public, she was the one who maintained control of the situation. That was when the Bag Man showed up. I didn't even know he was there at first. Not until he tried to put this ugly baseball cap on my head. I thought he was some bum or retarded guy interfering in our business. Then he put the same hat on my son. He didn't take it as well as I did, he threw the hat down and told him to leave, but not in a nice way. That's when the officers came on the scene and separated us.

"I didn't think much about it at the time, but I think when the Bag Man put that hat on John's head it transferred a spirit of forgiveness to him. I can't prove that, but early the next morning Margaret called me and said that they wanted to meet with me again. It was an answer to my prayers. The last couple of weeks have been hard, but we are working through it. Once again I can't prove it, but I think the Bag Man had something to do with me getting my son back in my life. I'm just sorry that I never got the chance to thank him for that."

When the gentleman finished talking, he went to stand by his son. All three of them had an emotional moment as they hugged each other.

While everyone was watching them hug, Officer Smith pulled a couple of items out of the bag and said, "This appears to be nothing but trash."

As she placed the trash on the table in front of her, I recognized some of it. It was the empty Subway sandwich wrapper and empty Coke bottle that the Bag Man gave to that old guy on the square. Nobody said anything at first, so Officer Smith said, "I guess he was hungry," and gave a little chuckle under her breath.

Before she could reach back into the bag somebody in the back of the room spoke up and said, "They are mine."

Everyone's attention diverted to the back of the room to see who it was. Out of the crowd stepped the old man from the square. He walked up to Officer Smith and took the trash from the table. He was an old, rugged, and somewhat ungroomed gentleman. He looked like someone who probably wouldn't fit in with most groups. He began to speak in a deep, humble voice.

"My name is Harry. I have been a homeless person for a while. I don't know how long. It started when my wife passed away about three years ago from cancer. We had no children because my wife had many medical problems over the years. It just worked out that way I guess. I worked in one of the mills here in town for a few years before my wife died, but when the economy got bad the mills closed down or moved out of town. I drew unemployment for a period of time, but the money quickly ran out because of the medical bills. We didn't have medical insurance; we couldn't afford it. I tried to find work, but no one was hiring. Besides, my wife was bad off and close to death, and I didn't want to leave her alone. After my wife died things began to get worse. Finally, the banks foreclosed on my home because I couldn't pay the mortgage. That is how I came to be homeless.

"Shortly afterward I began to see a man around town who called himself 'the Bag Man.' One day, after seeing him a few times, he stopped and asked me if I needed anything. I told him I was hungry. He simply said 'Okay,' turned and walked away. I just assumed that he was like most people who didn't want anything to do with a bum like me, so I didn't give him a second thought. A few minutes later, to my surprise, he came back with some food for me. I was touched by his actions because you just don't see that very often. He even sat down next to me and talked while I ate the food. He didn't talk at me like most people do, he talked with me. That felt wonderful! It made me feel like a real person again!

"I didn't see him every day, only on occasions when I felt really down and couldn't find anything to eat. He always showed up when I needed him most. I never was much of a religious kind of guy, but he always told me that our heavenly father would take care of things at the right time. I didn't pay him much attention about that kind of stuff because I blamed God for my wife dying. When I told him that it didn't change his mind, he just kept feeding me and being my friend. This went on for almost a year.

"The last time I saw him was about a week and half ago. I was having a hard time finding food. I was even being threatened by a restaurant owner. I was sitting down against the wall of a building on the square when he walked up. He asked me how I was doing then sat down next to me. He opened that bag and pulled out a Subway sandwich and a bottle of Coke. He gave them to me to eat and drink. I offered some of it to him, but he said he had already eaten and this was mine. He always said that. We had a great conversation that day filled with seriousness and laughter. When I finished eating, he asked for the sandwich wrapper and bottle back. He said he would take care of it later.

"We got up and walked down the street together. He wasn't ashamed of being seen with me. I think he enjoyed my company as much as I enjoyed his. As we were walking down the street he kept looking behind us at someone."

He pointed at me and said, "I think it was you. I asked him who you were, but he just said you were someone whom he was going to ask for help with a project in the future. Then he started talking about me again. Before he left me that night, the last thing he said to me was to not give up on God yet, because God hasn't given up on me. I never saw him again after that night.

"The next morning I was walking through the square as usual when the restaurant owner called me over to him. I quickly told him that I wasn't going to bother his place of business anymore. He asked me to come inside to talk. He fixed me breakfast. While I ate he talked to me. He said he had a proposition for me: If I would clean up around his place of business a little everyday, he would give me food to eat. I took him up on his offer and have been doing it for a week now.

"Yesterday he pulled me aside to talk again. I told him I was working very hard and hoped he hadn't changed his mind about our arrangement. He said that he did change his mind about me. I was very disappointed and was about to leave when he said that a man that carried a big bag came by last week.

"The restaurant owner said, 'He asked if I would give you a chance to prove your worth to me. He was convinced that you would do a great job if I helped you out with food. He was right. You do a great job. That is why I want to offer you a full-time job working for me in my restaurant. It's a hard job that most people don't want to do, like wash dishes, clean the toilet, mop the floor, and anything else I need done. But you have to clean yourself up a bit.'

"I explained to him that I was homeless and didn't have a way to clean myself up good enough. He told me not to worry about that because he and his wife had just finished fixing up their garage into a small apartment to rent out. He said it wasn't very big. It had only four small rooms: a living room, kitchen, bathroom, and bedroom. He said he would let me stay there as part of my pay. He said that the guy that told him about me went by the nickname Bag Man, because he always carried a big bag with him. I couldn't say anything to the guy offering me the job. I could only shake my head yes and cry.

"I start my new job tomorrow and have a place to live starting tonight. I owe all of this to my friend, the Bag Man. I'm not going to say that the Bag Man is God, but he sure was a messenger sent by God!"

The old man turned and walked back to the back of the room and continued to cry happy tears.

––––––––––––––

The atmosphere in the room had changed. It was now one of amazement and anticipation. Officer Smith pulled another item out of the bag. When she held it up and looked at it, it appeared to be a paper jacket cover to a large book. She turned it around and read the title of the book, *The New International Version Study Bible*.

A quiet and humble young lady who looked to be in her late twenties walked up and took the book cover from Officer Smith. Turning slowly to face the crowd, she began to speak. Her head was hanging down, and her eyes were facing the floor. She had a soft voice, one you had to really listen to in order to hear.

"My name is Nicole Brooks, and I have two children, a girl and a boy, two and five years old. About a year ago my husband abandoned me and the children. He just left one day and never came back. No explanation or anything. I hired people to look for him, but they had no results. I thought we would be fine without him, but it didn't work out that way. Then I got behind on the bills. To make things worse, I lost my job due to downsizing. I drew unemployment for a few weeks, but then the money ran out. I tried to find another job, but nobody was hiring. I couldn't pay the rent anymore. People were nice at first, but then the banks wanted their money. I didn't have any family to turn to for help. I became a desperate person when I realized that my kids might not have a place to sleep or call home.

"A couple of weeks ago, I met a guy who told me he knew a way I could make a lot of good money real fast. All I had to do was make a few men very happy. I knew what he meant and told him no way. He put his card in my shirt pocket and said if I changed my mind to give him a call. A few days later I got a notice in the mail that said if I didn't pay the bank within a week they would foreclose on my house and my kids and I would be on the streets. I panicked and became even more desperate. While I was getting my dirty clothes together, I found that card the man gave me.

I thought maybe I could find out exactly what he was talking about. So I called him.

"He picked me up and took me to a party outside of town. What I saw was a few young ladies being handed a lot of money. I needed some of that money, too, so I agreed to do whatever it took. I quickly found myself doing the same things those other ladies did. I did a lot of different things with a lot of different men for a lot of money, men that I didn't even know. I thought it would make a difference since the men were from out of town and they didn't know me either, but it didn't matter. I felt so guilty, so ashamed, and so dirty. I justified it in my mind as taking care of my kids, but on the inside I cried the whole time I was doing it. The next morning I walked away with two thousand dollars in my hands. It was enough money to pay so I could keep my house.

"That evening, I found myself walking around town thinking about what I had done. Every time I walked by someone that made eye contact with me, I felt like they knew what I had done. They couldn't know, but guilt made me believe they did. Again, I justified it in my mind as providing for my kids, but at what cost? Dignity was gone, replaced by guilt, and my self-esteem turned to shame. That night I gave away my soul and was left with nothing but an empty shell inside.

"I found myself sitting on a bench by the fountain on the square. All I could do was blankly stare into my own soul, replaying every scene from the night before.

With each passing moment I felt more guilt and more shame fill me. I must have sat there for hours.

"After a while a man came and sat down beside me on the bench. He put his arm around me, and I thought it was just another man wanting something from me. After he pulled my head down to his shoulder I realized that he was different. He wasn't there to get something from me; he was there to give something to me. I sat there for a few minutes with my head on his shoulder, and for the first time in a long time, I felt safe. On the outside I showed no emotions at all, but on the inside I was crying my heart out!

"After a few minutes, when I was ready, he started whispering things into my ear. They were encouraging things like 'God still loves you, you are special, and God has a destiny planned just for you.'

After a couple of minutes of whispering in my ear, he moved my head from his shoulder. He reached into his bag and pulled out a large book. He opened it and started reading to me. What he read said that if I confessed my sins to the Lord, that He is faithful to forgive me and clean me from all of the ugly, dirty, and sinful things in my life. He lifted his head and looked directly into my eyes. He continued talking to me, but I don't remember anything else he said. His eyes saw past my eyes deep inside of me. He was no longer speaking into my ears. Instead he was speaking to the very core of my soul! I can't explain it. I just know it happened.

"Then without hesitating he gave me the book, grabbed his bag, and walked away. I opened the book and found a piece of paper with a woman's name, address, and phone number written on it. I quickly left and found the address and knocked on the door. When the door opened I saw a very confident-looking woman standing there. I introduced myself and told her that I had no idea who she was, but I found her name and address inside a book. I felt like I was supposed to talk to her. She introduced herself as the pastor's wife of a prominent church in the area. I had heard of the church before but didn't know anything about it.

"After talking for a few minutes, I found myself telling her what had happened the night before and how I felt. I was bearing my soul to her. When I finished bearing my soul to her she pulled me into her arms and held me tight as I bitterly and openly wept. The whole time I heard this woman, who had never met me before, cry with me. It was as if she was hurting with me and for me. When we regained our composure, she opened up her bible and began to read to me. It was the same thing that the Bag Man read to me, and I told her so. She asked me if I wanted to change. I told her I did. She held me again and began to pray for me. I simply and softly asked God to forgive me and make me clean again. I didn't scream or pray loud. I didn't jump up and down. I didn't even cry again. I had already cried as much as I could. I just honestly asked God for forgiveness. As I was praying, I felt the guilt leave my heart. The depression left me along with the shame, and a peace come over me like I had never felt before. I felt clean again. It was as if I became a brand-new person! The pastor's wife called it 'getting saved and being born again.' All I knew was I wanted to stay that way.

"Before I left that house I gave the woman the two thousand dollars I had from the night before and told her that I didn't want it anymore, it was dirty money. I told her to do something good with it. When I left that house I felt like my life had a new beginning. I didn't know what I was going to do about my house. All I knew was that somehow we were going to be okay.

"The next morning, after the kids went to school, there was a knock on the door. When I opened the door, there stood the pastor's wife from the evening before. Before I could say a word she looked at me and said 'When God cleaned you up, he cleaned the money also. Get your purse, and let's go to the bank.'

"That day God provided a new life and a fresh start for my family, and he started the whole process with the Bag Man. Without him I would still be sitting on that bench an unclean person."

The woman confidently walked back to take her place in the crowd with a new purpose and new resolve.

———

When Officer Smith pulled the next item out of the bag, she held it up for everyone to see. I recognized it as the handkerchief that the Bag Man gave to the beautiful high society lady that was sitting on the bench and crying about two weeks ago. But somehow it looked different. I couldn't place my finger on what it was, but something was different. Suddenly that beautiful lady stepped out of the crowd and walked up front. She took the handkerchief and lightly brushed it against her cheek, it was as if she was remembering that night on the square. She turned to face the crowd and began to speak.

"My name is Sarah Willingham. I met the Bag Man almost two weeks ago. My husband was working late again and I had nothing to do, so I drove to the square and decided to go for a walk. I don't know how long I walked around, but I found myself sitting down on a bench next to the fountain. Everything seemed great in my life, at least that's how it appeared on the outside. I felt and looked like a trophy wife. I had money, diamonds, good looks, a great car, and a mansion to live in. It was everything that most women would die for. But something was missing on the inside. The life I was living was like a fantasy on the outside but torment on the inside. My marriage was falling apart, and I was scared.

"While sitting on that bench that night, I was literally at my wit's end. I had no idea what to do. I was trying to keep my proper composure, but when you are hurting that bad it will show. I cried so much. That was nothing new to me; I did that a lot anyway. But that night I cried my heart out. I cried so much that my eyes were swelled shut, my nose was running, and my face was streaked with mascara. I was a mess compared to my normal appearance.

"Without warning, a voice started speaking to me. It was a deep voice but very clear. The voice encouraged me a great deal, but also told me to let all of it out of my heart. I felt a touch on my hand, so I opened my eyes enough to see a man kneeling before me. I had never seen him before, but I didn't care. He put this handkerchief in my hand, and I buried my face into it and cried with all of my might. You can say what you will, but I believe it was God himself talking to me! He knew things I felt and things about me that I have never spoken of to anyone for fear I would lose what I had. He also spoke of private and personal things meant for my ears only that no one needs to know details about.

"As he spoke, he told me what to do. I didn't want to at first, but he told me things would get worse if I didn't. He said, 'Have faith, my child, only believe.'

"I told the voice that I would do it. Suddenly a peace swept over my soul like never before. I got up and hugged him. It was an overwhelming hug that engulfed my entire existence. I felt like I was hugging God! I gave him this handkerchief back and walked to my car. While driving home I felt nervous and afraid, but I knew what I must do."

As the lady stood there she focused her attention toward someone else as she held out her hands in that direction. From the corner of the room a man stepped out. As society would say, he was a very handsome man with a good physique, and was wearing a very nice suit and tie. He had that look of a businessman that you would see on the front of a magazine cover. He also looked familiar to me. I had seen him before, I just didn't remember where. As the man walked toward the woman I looked over at the pile of magazines stacked on top of the coffee table. The top magazine was the *Businessman's Quarterly Magazine* that I subscribe to. I kid you not that the man standing in front of my living room was the man on the cover of that magazine! I motioned to my wife to pick up the magazine. Her eyes grew bigger and her mouth opened and she gasped as she, too, realized it was him. The man saw us out of the corner of his eye. He gently kissed the woman on the cheek and walked over to where we were standing. He saw the magazine in my wife's hand and said, "May I?"

My wife handed him the magazine, and he walked back to the woman. She took hold of his hand and introduced him as her husband. He kissed her hand as he let go of it, and took a step forward. He held up the magazine and began to speak.

"My name is Ronald Willingham, and this is about me. The title of the article is 'Success At Any Cost.' I am a very successful business man, and this story described me to a 'T.' You just heard what my wife told you about her experience with the Bag Man. With her permission, I would like to tell the rest of the story."

He turned and looked toward his wife. With a huge smile on her face and rays of bliss glowing from her eyes she quickly said, "Please do so!" The man continued to speak.

"About two weeks ago, on the same night my wife told you about, I came home from work late as usual. My wife was sitting on the couch, all elegant and beautiful as she always is. As I entered the room, I could tell something wasn't right by the look on her face. She motioned for me to sit next to her, and she said we needed to talk. Like most men would, I cringed when she said that. As I sat next to her she began to tell me how unhappy she was with our marriage. I came unglued when she said that. I lost my composure and angrily said some things I probably shouldn't have said.

"As we continued our little talk, I became defensive with my statements. 'I worked very hard and very long to provide for you. I bought you diamonds, I bought you good cars, I bought you the best clothes, and I bought you this huge mansion. For God's sake, what more do you want from me? Just tell me, and I will buy it for you!'

"'I have the clothes, I have the cars, I have the diamonds and the house, but I don't have you. I want you!' she said.

"'You think I'm having an affair. I have never been unfaithful to you with anyone!'

"'I have never believed that for one second. But your work has become your mistress.'

"'I have to work to pay for all of this stuff for you. I work so hard to buy you these things to prove I love you. Isn't that what husbands are supposed to do?'

"After pacing the floor for a few minutes, trying to figure out what she was trying to tell me, and why she felt this way, I calmed down and sat back down on the couch next to her. She slid herself down to the floor on her knees and pulled herself close to me. She looked into my eyes and with a gentle voice began to talk again.

"'I know you love me, and I appreciate and enjoy you getting me all of this stuff, but you haven't even been intimate with me in a long time, almost a year now!'

"'Is that what this is all about, being intimate with you? I can do that more often!'

"'Although I need that from you on an extreme and intense level, more than you know, I want my whole husband back. Your job has become the most important thing in your life. I want and I need to be number one in your life again. And it hasn't been that way for a long time. I can't live like this anymore. I need to be number one or not at all.'

"'But I thought I was putting you number one by getting you all of these things?'

"'I enjoy all of these things, but it means nothing to me if I can't enjoy them with you. I need to enjoy my husband, all of him, and I need my husband to enjoy his wife, all of her! Without that, it's just stuff.'

"As the conversation continued, we worked out our feelings. It's amazing what you can learn if you just stop and listen. The next day I called work and told them I was going out of town for a while. I can do that because I own the company and I'm the boss. We took a little vacation away from everything. Nothing elaborate, just time together. It was like a honeymoon all over again. We got to know and enjoy one another again, the laughter, the time, the conversations, the atmosphere, and especially the times of intimacy together. We became a couple again. Don't get me wrong, we still have issues and responsibilities to work out, but we will get there together.

"When we got back home, I called the editor of the *Businessman's Quarterly Magazine* and set up a new interview. This time it was with both of us talking about the pros and cons of what success will cost. As we settled into our new life together, we read the article about the Bag Man dying. That is what brought us here today. Though I never got the chance to meet him, he has made a huge difference in my life now, and in the future to come."

As they started to walk back into the crowd, I approached them and quietly told them that I witnessed her with the Bag Man that night and that there was more they needed to hear, but it was just for them and no one else. I told them to call me and we could have dinner or something and the four of us could talk privately.

Before I could finish talking with the Willinghams, Officer Smith had already taken another item out of the duffel bag. I hadn't even seen what it was yet when someone in the crowd whispered in a soft voice, "*Oh my God!*"

It was enough to get my attention refocused. Officer Smith was holding up a couple of handfuls of mangled material. Once again I recognized what they were. They were the two bandages the Bag Man put around the wheelchair guy's legs. As that guy began to walk toward Officer Smith, I was particularly interested in what this guy had to say. I didn't understand what I saw, but maybe this guy could shed some light on it.

"My name is Terry Wells, and I used to be a cripple. For fifteen years I was confined to a wheelchair. I was paralyzed from my upper thighs down. I didn't even have any feelings in my legs. It was a difficult way to live. As you can see, I can now walk as well as anyone.

"Fifteen years ago, at the age of sixteen, I got my driver's license like most people do. I was a pretty good driver too. My father taught me well. The very next day we went for dinner to celebrate me getting my license. It was a Friday night about nine p.m. The weather was good, and the moon was bright. I was driving home from the restaurant, proud as could be.

"Suddenly, out of nowhere, a car came toward us. It was swerving back and forth into our lane. I did all of the defensive driving I could remember, but it was obvious that we would be hit. The only thing I could think of was to swerve onto the shoulder of the road. When the other car passed, I tried to get back onto the road, but I overcompensated and the car began to flip over. It flipped over several times before it came to a stop upside down. It knocked me out cold. I was sedated because of my injuries, and it was several days before I woke up. It was then that I was told that both of my parents had died from the accident and that I would be paralyzed from the thighs down. It was the worst day of my life. An officer came by later and explained that it was a drunk driver that ran me off of the road and that he had been caught and put in jail for a long time. That was good news, but it still wouldn't bring back my parents.

"I stayed with other family members, and they took care of me. I was a bitter teenager who blamed himself for his parents' deaths. I couldn't help but think if I wasn't driving that night they might still be alive. Months later I was awarded a large settlement from the insurance company of the drunk driver. When I turned eighteen years old, I moved to my own place and learned to live life with my disabilities. On occasion I found myself in difficult situations, especially dealing with decisions and emotions I was facing. I simply asked myself, 'What would mom say, or what would dad do?' That helped me make good decisions, plus it helped me keep them alive in my head.

"A few days ago, I was at the square. I used to go there a lot because looking at the fountain and feeding the birds helped me forget about reality for a brief period of time. It was like a small window of relief. I learned to cope with life by doing little insignificant things like that. Little did I know that day my destiny would reveal itself to me.

"I rolled my wheelchair to the normal spot where I fed the birds. Somebody else was there first. I started to move to a different place, but the man, now known as the Bag Man, offered me some bread to feed the birds. It was an invitation to join him. So I did.

"After about ten minutes of sitting there quietly feeding the birds, he turned and focused his attention on me. He pointed toward my wheelchair and said, 'What's up with your legs?'

"At first I was a little put off and offended by his question. How could this man, who I have never met before or even spoken to, ask such a bold and personal question? After a few seconds to ponder my response, I thought, 'What the heck, if he's bold enough to ask, I'll be bold enough to answer.' I started telling him my story.

"After a couple of minutes it was difficult to speak, because it had been years since I had even spoken about it, and now I was forced to face emotions and guilt and questions inside that had never been resolved. Tears began to flow down my face as I continued to tell the story. Instinctively, I began to rub my legs because they were hurting. I didn't realize it at the time, but now that I think about it, that moment must have been when it all started, because from the time of the accident till then, there had been no feeling in my legs at all. Not even pain! I finished telling my story, and we sat there silently.

"After a couple of minutes or so, the Bag Man asked another question.

"'What would you do if you could walk again?'

"I responded with a question of my own, 'You don't think that somehow you're pushing your luck with these questions, do you?'

"'No, I'm serious. If you could walk again, what would you do?'

"'Well, I've never given it much thought. I guess I never had a reason to think it could happen. If it couldn't happen, why think about it?'

"The Bag Man got off of the bench and knelt down in front of me. He pulled his duffel bag down beside him. I could see and feel him rolling up my pants legs. I asked,

'What are you doing?'

"'Don't worry about that right now. Just answer the question. What would you do if you could walk again?'

"'Well, I guess I would help other people who were in wheelchairs.'

"'How can you help other people in wheelchairs if you are in one yourself?'

"'I thought you said I could walk. If I could walk, I wouldn't be in a wheelchair anymore.'

"'That would mean that you no longer have anything in common with other people in wheelchairs. If that's so, how could you help them?'

"'I could help them because I've been where they are now. I've felt their pain, I've felt their anger. I had their disability. I know how they feel and how to cope with it. I have the experience.'

"Before I knew it he had wrapped both of my legs with some kind of bandages. I had no idea why he did that.

"'Why are you doing that?' I asked.

"'Don't ask, just focus on the conversation. Tell me again why you think you can do it and be successful with it.'

"'Because I've been where they are.'

"'I don't know! You still have a lot of emotions and questions to work out. Dude, you've got a boatload of baggage!'

"At that point the Bag Man had taken the bandages off of my legs and was sitting on the bench again.

"'I still don't know if you can do it.'

"'I can!'

"'What if you can't?'

"'Then I'll get somebody to help me do it.'

"'I don't know.'

"'I need to help them. *I want the chance!*'

"After a few seconds of hesitation, the Bag Man slapped his hands on his legs and said, 'Well, okay then. That's all I needed to hear. Let's do it!'

"The Bag Man stood up in front of me and held out his hands moving them in an upward motion.

"'Get up.'"

"'What?'"

"'I said stand up. Right now!'

"My legs were weak at first, so he helped me stand up. Then he let go of my hands. I found myself standing without help. It scared me, so I started to sit back down in my wheelchair. He grabbed my arm and wouldn't let me sit down, saying, 'Now, walk with me.'

"I put my arm in his, and he helped me walk to the end of the bench and back. We turned around, and he let go of my arm. He moved to the end of the bench and said, 'Walk to me again.'

"I steadied myself by hanging on to the bench as I walked, but I made it. He backed up another ten feet and motioned with his hands, 'Now walk to me without any help.'

"He repeated the process over and over and over again, for almost half an hour. By the time he was finished, I was walking on my own and even skipping a little. Now look at me, I can walk, run, and jump without any problems. It was a true miracle!

"Before I left the Bag Man that day, I gave him the biggest hug and thank you possible. After we finished crying, he started laughing. I haven't experienced that kind of joy since I got my driver's license. He looked with approval and said, 'Don't forget your promise.' I told him I wouldn't.

"After that day I never saw him again. I am making arrangements to start a program helping boys and girls in wheelchairs. It's not much, but it's a start. I intend on keeping my promise."

Terry Wells walked back into the crowd a new man with new skills. He was a man with a new mission. A mission that would be difficult, but somehow I knew it was his destiny. A few people in the crowd even clapped their hands in celebration of his new life.

After Officer Smith pulled the next item out of the bag it seemed a little less important. She held it up and asked, "Does anyone know anything about this receipt from the dollar store?"

She began to read the items on the receipt. I immediately knew it was the items that the Bag Man bought and gave away. When no one responded, Officer Smith laid it down on the table and proceeded to reach into the bag for another item. Before she could pull the next item out, a man spoke and said, "No, wait. It was for me."

A very large man stepped forward and picked up the receipt. As he turned to face the people, he began to speak in a low, deep voice.

"My name is James. This might not sound like much compared to the stories you've heard so far, but it was a life-changing event for me. A couple of years ago my wife passed away from cancer. We only had enough insurance to pay for her burial. We didn't think we would ever have to deal with anything like that for a long time. After she died it cut the household income in half. We had a three-year-old daughter that was devastated because she no longer had a mother to talk to.

"After a while hospital bills had piled up, and the house payment increased. I lost the house and found myself and my daughter living in my car. Eventually my job was phased out. I picked up side jobs for a while until I found a good job again. By that time somebody had already called the Division of Family and Children Services. After investigating me, they found it unsafe for my daughter to live like that, so they took her from me and put her in the foster care system. I was able to visit her with supervision, but was not allowed to take her anywhere or be with her unsupervised. However, the judge did say I could possibly get her back in the future if I maintained a proper job and a decent living environment. At the time, that seemed like something that could never happen.

"About a week ago, this guy, whom I've never met before, knocked on my car window and woke me up. I now know it was the Bag Man, but I had never seen him before or after that night. When I got out of the car and stood facing him I was looking down at him because I'm such a tall man of six foot and nine inches.

"He started talking and asked me, very politely, not to interrupt him until he was finished. During that time he told me everything in detail that had happened to me over the last two years. I asked him how he knew those things, and he simply replied, 'My father knows everything about you and your daughter.'

"At that point he opened his duffel bag and pulled a white bag out of it. He opened it and showed me the contents and then tried to give it to me. Being the proud man that I am, I didn't want to take the stuff. He just looked up at me and said, 'My child, I can't help you if you won't let me.'

"There was no denying the fact that God was speaking to me. I took the bag from him. He shook my hand and walked away without saying another word.

"When I got back in my car, I was so overwhelmed that all I could do was cry. That was different for me because I have always been a man full of pride. When

I opened that bag and looked inside, there was a newspaper opened to the 'Help Wanted' section. One of the ads was circled in red ink. It was an ad looking for someone interested in renting a garage apartment. Suddenly it became clear in my spirit what I needed to do.

"I drove to the nearest store I could find with restrooms. I spent some time cleaning myself up. I shaved, washed my hair and my body as much as possible, brushed my teeth, and put on those new clothes that were given to me. When I left there I went straight to the address in the ad.

"When I got there I met a very nice elderly lady. She invited me in to talk. She seemed interested in renting the apartment to me. At that point I felt it necessary to be honest with her, so I told her everything that had happened over the last two years, including my daughter. She told me that she felt like someone would rent her place that night and before I even came by she felt a peace about it. Even after me telling her the complete truth, she said she still had peace that I was the one to rent the apartment. It was an answer to my prayer.

"The next day I went down to DFCS and talked with my daughter's case worker. She said that they would investigate further, and if everything checked out after three months, they would consider giving me legal custody of my daughter again, but only if they felt it would be best for my daughter. I know, somehow, that everything will work out and I will have my daughter back at the right time. I wish I had the opportunity to tell the Bag Man how things turned out, but for some reason I never saw him again. I think he had it planned all along and all I needed was the right one to push me that way. Maybe, just maybe, he already knows!"

As James started walking back to his seat my wife stepped forward and said, "If it's okay with everyone, I think it would be a good time to take a restroom break. Be back here in about fifteen minutes." Officer Smith agreed with her.

As everyone gathered back into the living room, Officer Smith continued searching the duffel bag. The next item she pulled from the bag was a very large item compared to the ones so far. I didn't recognize what it was right away. It was only after it was unfolded that I could tell what it was. It was a long black overcoat. I remembered the Bag Man wearing it only once. It was with the teenager at the fountain. Just as that thought crossed my mind, that very girl stepped out and walked forward. She was crying as she took the overcoat from Officer Smith. She buried her face into the coat until she finished crying. Once she faced the crowd, she put on the overcoat and started her story.

"My name is Tiffany Brown, and these are my parents Debbie and Rick Brown. About a month ago I met this guy who I liked a lot. Right away, my parents didn't like him and even tried to keep me from seeing him. They said his type was nothing but trouble. I didn't believe them. I wanted to believe in love at first sight. I thought I loved him, and he told me he loved me, too. I got tired of my parents treating me like a kid, because I thought I was all grown up.

"One night I had an argument with my parents. After they went to bed I crawled out of my window and ran away with him. The next morning my parents tried to call me, but he took my cell phone away and broke it, saying all they wanted to do was cause trouble. Everything was great for about a week. Then things changed.

"He tried to get me to do drugs with him, but I wouldn't do it. I've never done drugs before, and didn't want to start then. He started seeing other girls while he was seeing me. When I confronted him about it, all he said was, 'That's the way it's done here; everybody shares everything with everybody else. We are one big happy family. Drugs, sex, and fast cars: that's our motto.'

"I told him I wasn't raised that way, but all he would say was, 'Get used to it. That's the way it is now.'

"That was when I realized I was in way over my head, and I didn't know what to do. My parents were right; he was not good for me. I wished I had listened to them, but it was too late now. I waited until he passed out from drinking so much, and then I snuck out and never went back. I walked around town for a couple of days and had a couple of friends from school that let me sleep at their house. I was all alone and didn't know what to do.

"One evening I was walking around town, trying to figure out what to do next. My mind wasn't thinking straight. I sat down by the fountain and finally broke down emotionally. Many people walked by and just stared at me. I didn't care who saw me or what they thought. All I knew for sure was that I wasn't going back to him!

"That's when the Bag Man approached me. I didn't know who he was at the time, but he seemed to have a safe spirit about him. It was getting colder as the night grew longer, so he took off this overcoat and put it on my shoulders. It felt so warm and safe. Even though I didn't know him, it felt like he knew me. I told him everything I had done and everything I wouldn't do and how I ended up on the street that night.

"When I finished talking he told me about a guy he called 'The Prodigal Son.' When he finished telling the story, I realized that I was the prodigal daughter. He asked me if I thought my parents loved me. I told him I did. They had told me in the past that they might not approve of what I do or say, but I was still their daughter and they would always love me. But this time I said some mean things to them and hurt them a lot. I really screwed up big time!

"He looked at me and said, 'I think they are a little upset with you, but I know they are more worried about you and your safety. That is their main concern. They have talked to me many times while you've been gone. They just want you back home and safe with them. They love you more than you think they do.

Why don't we go find a phone and call them, that way you can find out for yourself? If they say no, at least you will know for sure.'

"The Bag Man really made a lot of sense. After giving it a little thought, I wanted to call them, but I was scared of what they might say. I didn't know what I would do if they said no. He told me not to worry about it, if they said no he would take care of me.

"We left the square to look for a phone. The closest one was down the road at the drugstore, so we walked there. The whole time we were walking, he was telling me stories about people who thought they had ruined their lives forever, but his father always worked it out for them. He seemed to know everything about a lot of people. As we were walking I kept seeing somebody who looked like he was following us. I told the Bag Man, and he wasn't worried about it. He didn't even look back to see who it was. He just said, 'Don't worry about him; he's one of the good guys.'

"It was like he already knew the guy was there.

"When we reached the drugstore, we went inside to use the pay phone. He took some change out of his pocket and put it in the coin slot. I was so nervous and shaking so much that I couldn't even push the buttons on the panel. The Bag Man had to dial the number for me. The phone rang only once before someone answered.

"'Hello.'

"'Mom, it's me Tiffany.'

"'Oh my God! Are you all right?'

"'I'm fine.'

"I tried to fight back the tears as we were talking, but I couldn't help myself. I was crying like a baby, and so was my mom.

"'Mom, I'm so sorry for what I did. I was wrong, can you forgive me?'

"'Of course I forgive you, honey.'

"'I'm scared and want to come home. Can I come home?'

"'Yes, I want you at home with me. Where are you?'

"'I'm at the drugstore in town.'

"'Stay there. We are on our way!'

"'Mom?'

"'Yes, honey?'

"'Do you still love me after all I've done?'

"'Honey, we have never stopped loving you, and we never will!'

"'I love you too, Mom.'

"When I hung up the phone, I turned to the Bag Man and thanked him for helping me. He pulled me close and held me tightly, and as I continued to cry, he cried with me. I was still scared, but happy at the same time. I took off the overcoat and gave it back to him. About that time he motioned toward the parking lot. As I turned to look, I saw my dad's car pull in. I walked out of the store and into the parking lot. As the back door opened for me to get inside, I hesitated. I wanted to say good-bye to the Bag Man one more time, but as I looked around he was nowhere to be found. During the ride home, no one said a word. My mother just held me in her arms, and we both cried the whole time.

"That night I slept like a baby, safe and warm at home. The next day we talked a lot about what happened and why. I found a new respect for my parents and their rules. They are put there for a reason, whether I agree with them or not. I let them down and need to regain their trust. But I now know that I can trust them. They are smarter than I gave them credit for. And the most important thing of all, they love me no matter what!

"I tried to find the Bag Man again but was unsuccessful. But he did leave me with a better understanding of true unconditional love. Dad told me that the stories the Bag Man told me were straight from the Bible. I knew they sounded familiar. I just didn't know why. I found those stories in the Bible and read all of them again. It's strange though, when the Bag Man told me those stories, it sounded like he was there when they happened. But how could that be? Those stories are thousands of years old. I can't explain it. All I know is that he was there for me when I needed someone. And I thank him for that!"

Tiffany's words created a lot of emotion in my wife. I could see tears as they started to stream down her face. I could tell they were different from normal tears. They were a mother's tears. If I knew my wife like I think I did, she was thinking about how she would feel if that was our daughter.

What Officer Smith pulled out of the bag next appeared like normal trash to most people, but I knew what it was. It was my old sweat towel with an empty water bottle rolled up inside of it. My wife recognized it as my towel from the initials on it. It was a towel she had made for me. My wife turned and faced me with that odd "I have a question" look on her face. I knew she wanted to know how my towel got in that bag. I figured it would come out in someone's story, so I just shrugged my shoulders. She didn't like that very much.

A young lady, who I didn't recognize, stepped out of the group and walked up front to where Officer Smith was standing. She took the towel and empty bottle from her, then turned to face the crowd. She started her story.

"My name is Brandi Collins. This isn't normal trash, to me its pure gold! As you can tell by the scars and needle marks on my arms, I'm a drug addict. Let me re-phrase that, I'm a former drug addict.

Her eyes scanned the crowd briefly until they found Tiffany and they focused on her.

"Tiffany, I started off making the same mistake you did. I ran away with a guy too, only I didn't have guts enough to leave him. He got me involved with drugs, and I quickly became addicted to them. After a while he started to use that against me. He made me do a lot of bad things just to get my fix. It took me deeper and deeper into a life I didn't want to be in, a lifestyle of guilt, shame, and disgust. I did anything and everything they wanted just so I could get my drugs. It had a hold on me that I just couldn't break.

"I don't remember much about my encounter with the Bag Man, only that somebody else was with him. I had an argument with my drug dealer. I told him I didn't want to do those bad things anymore, but I still wanted the drugs. He didn't like that and started beating me real bad. I think he would have killed me if the Bag Man hadn't shown up to help me. It's all fuzzy in my head, and I only remember bits and pieces of what happened, but here is what I know for sure.

"The Bag Man kept stepping between me and the drug dealer. He wouldn't let the drug dealer get to me, or me to the drug dealer. I knew the dealer pretty well. He was bad news and had no problem killing anybody that got in his way. I've seen him do it! That night the Bag Man literally stood as my protector. He stood between me and certain death.

"The next thing I remember was the Bag Man holding me in his arms. I wanted to give up and die, but all I could hear was him whispering in my ear. One statement kept me fighting, 'You can make it. I know you can!'

"He kept saying that over and over again. Throughout the night I fought withdrawal from the drugs and the desire to die. He just kept whispering in my ear. Occasionally he would wet this towel with water from this bottle and wipe my face with it. He literally saved my life.

"I'm still having some issues with the shakes caused by withdrawal from the drugs, but I've gotten help from rehab and other people who have been where I was. It will be hard, but I keep hearing the Bag Man whispering in my ear, 'You can make it. I know you can!' I don't know why he chose to help me that night, but I'm glad he did!"

When Brandi finished talking, Tiffany walked up, and they hugged each other and cried on each other's shoulder. It was so beautiful! They finally moved back into the group so others wouldn't be distracted.

Officer Smith pulled another item out of the bag and unfolded it. It was a small blanket. My wife recognized it also as the one the Bag Man used the day we watched him together. She was excited to see a well-dressed gentleman walk forward toward the front of the room and pick up the blanket.

"My name is Jeff Smallwood. What happened to me was not so much a thing that you could see, as far as miracles are concerned. But to me it was still amazing!

"I didn't know the Bag Man as much as some of you did. I had seen him around town doing some good things for people, but never actually met the guy until four days ago. Even then it was brief. I haven't done any real bad things in my life, but haven't done anything good either.

"I am married, but I'm not the best husband I could be. I have two kids, but I'm not the best dad I should be. I have a very good job, but I don't do the quality of work I know I can do. I wasn't a bad guy, but still I knew I could be better. For some reason I wasn't all that I could be. It was like a battle going on inside my head. On the one hand I was going through all of the motions and doing the right things. On the other hand there was something missing inside. It felt like a big hole in my heart. I faked it for a long time. I smiled a lot and never had any confrontations with anyone. I fooled a lot of people.

"One day my mind just snapped. I thought of ending it all by killing myself. Even then people complimented me on how well they thought I was doing. I can't explain it, but I was full of guilt and shame, and didn't know why. I walked to the square that evening and found a place where I thought I wouldn't be seen. Finally, I couldn't take it anymore and broke down. Call it what you want, a breakdown or a meltdown, either way I shut down mentally.

"To my surprise the Bag Man approached me. He stooped down to talk and said some hard things to me. I informed him that I wasn't a bad person, but he simply replied, 'I know.'

'He pulled this blanket out of his bag a wrapped it around me and over my head. I think he was trying not to embarrass me. He told me things about myself and things I had done that no one else could have known. He explained that only Jesus Christ could take away the guilt and shame I was feeling, He was the only one who could fill that empty hole in my heart.

"Finally, he asked me if I wanted Jesus to help me. I thought what could it hurt? He prayed with me, and I asked Jesus to help me and fill the empty hole in my heart. Immediately, I felt changed. Somehow I was different. I went home and told my wife what happened. She said she had been praying for that to happen. I didn't know what it all meant, so she had to explain it all to me. I still don't understand everything completely. All I know is that I am a different person now, thanks to the Bag Man. I never got a chance to talk to him again and explain how he helped me. Somehow, I think he already knows."

It was getting late, so Officer Smith quickly pulled another item from the bag and laid it on the table. It was an article of clothing. Smith again searched the bag and also laid it on the table. She refocused on the clothing. When she unfolded it, I immediately knew what it was, but I wasn't the only one who recognized it. It was the shirt that the Bag Man was wearing the night he died. It was soaked with blood in several areas.

Suddenly someone quickly stepped from the crowd and took the shirt from Officer Smith. It was the woman from the square that had been stabbed in the chest. She buried her face in the bloody shirt and began to weep uncontrollably. When she regained her emotions, she turned and faced the crowd. Still focused on the shirt, she began to speak.

"My name is Brenda Fisher, and I had a life-changing encounter with the Bag Man. I am alive today because he is dead. He died in my place. Let me explain myself.

"Friday evening I was supposed to meet my husband, Lamar, for dinner at the steak house just off the square. It was crowded, so I had to park down the street. As I was walking to the restaurant, a man in a hooded sweatshirt jumped in front of me and grabbed my purse. My first instinct was to pull back on the straps. I had gotten paid that day and didn't want to lose my money. I know now that was a dumb thing to do, but at the time I didn't think about that. I just reacted. As the man pulled harder I screamed for help at the top of my lungs. A man from across the square screamed back and told him to stop. That just made the thief mad. He put his hand in his pocket and pulled out a knife. Before I could react, he stabbed me in the chest. As I fell to the ground he was able to pull my purse from my hands and run away.

"What happened next sounds like something you would read in a book, but I promise it really happened. I had what you might call an out-of-body experience. It was like I was floating in the air, watching everything from above. The first one to approach me was the Bag Man. He checked my pulse to see if I was still alive. After that he started talking to me. I know you may think I'm crazy here, but as I looked from above and beside him, he never moved his lips or opened his mouth. It was like he was talking directly into my soul with his mind. It wasn't scary, but instead it was soothing. Even though it was a complete conversation that happened in only a split second, I don't even remember what he said.

"The Bag Man took off his shirt and tried to stop the bleeding but was unsuccessful. Suddenly he pressed his shirt down on the open wound with extreme force. Afterward, he got up and left me there. My spirit began to spiral back down and entered my body again. The next thing I remember is the paramedics working on me trying to find out what happened.

"I can't explain what happened. All I know is that I got stabbed and that there was a knife sticking out of my chest."

She turned and stared at me, saying, "You know what I'm talking about. You were there. You saw the whole thing! On the way to the hospital I overheard the paramedics talking. They were saying the other man had died from what looked like a stab wound to the chest. I don't know how to explain it any other way, except he changed places with me. He died so that I could live. I don't know why he did that for me, but he did!"

As Brenda Fisher walked back into the group, Officer Smith picked up the duffel bag and looked inside one more time and said, "Well, that's everything from the bag. Thank you."

I stepped up to her and took the bag and looked inside. Yes, it was empty. I asked if I could have the bag. She nodded her head yes. I turned to face the group and began to speak. I told them I wanted to meet with them individually to talk about what I saw concerning each of them. They agreed. After exchanging numbers and information, everyone left for the night.

day

FOURTEEN

PART THREE

It was almost eleven o'clock when everyone finally left. I sat down in my recliner and searched the bag one more time. My wife started the conversation, "What are you looking for, honey?"

"I don't know. I guess I'm a little disappointed that there wasn't anything for me in the bag."

"At least you got his duffel bag. That's got to mean something, doesn't it?"

"Maybe you're right. I'm just being over emotional. But I just think I was supposed to learn something through all of this."

"Don't worry too much. You'll figure it out in time."

She kissed me on the cheek and started cleaning up. After a few minutes she came back in the living room and sat down. She picked up the bag and started spraying it with a deodorizing spray, saying it smelled bad. In the process of doing that she felt something in the lining of the bag. She put down the spray and started looking inside of it. She said she felt something inside the lining and wanted to see what it was. She found an overlapping pocket that I hadn't noticed earlier. She put her hand inside the pocket and pulled something out and handed it to me. It appeared to be an envelope. I unfolded the envelope and saw my name, Peter Stonewall, written on the front of it. I just sat there for a minute, staring at the envelope. I was actually nervous about opening it up.

My wife, Elizabeth, broke the silence, "Go ahead. Open it up and see what it says."

"I'm kind of afraid to."

"Well, you've come this far, don't let a little fear stop you now."

My hands were shaking so much that I could barely read the letter. Actually, it was more like him speaking to my soul than me reading what was written on paper. I heard his voice as if he were reading the letter to me.

> Dear Peter,
> If you are reading this letter, it means I'm not there with you anymore. I know you have a lot of questions, but I can't answer them all with a single letter. There is a reason why I chose to involve you, and only you, in my daily activities. Some things I can reveal to you now, but some things I can't. You're just going to have to trust me on some things.
> I have been watching you for some time. You have skills and talents inside of you that

you are just now beginning to tap into. That wasn't an accident; it was planned from the beginning. For the past few years you have been sitting by on the sidelines watching the world go by. You were very comfortable because it didn't require any effort from you. But now, the time has come for you to step into your destiny. A destiny planned just for you! It wasn't just circumstances that brought us together.

All of the people that you saw me help are part of your destiny also. Only, they don't know it yet. Yes, they have a destiny of their own, but they all involve you. They can't do it alone. They need a guide. They need a leader. They need you. You are that leader! Lead my people, and teach them my ways. That is your *destiny!*

When I finished reading the letter, I didn't know how to react. Elizabeth asked me what it said; I handed the letter to her so she could read it. When she finished the letter, she spoke first.

"Wow! What are you going to do?"

"I don't know. I still have a lot of questions that the letter didn't answer."

"Maybe the answers will come as you go along."

"What do you think I should do?"

"I can't answer that for you. You have to decide what you want to do. Just know that whatever you decide, I will be there by your side. I suggest you think hard about this and pray a lot. I will do the same for you."

Elizabeth kissed me and went upstairs to bed. She knew that I wouldn't be up anytime soon. I had to work some things out in my head. I just sat there for a while, pondering the many questions I had and playing out different scenes that I shared with the Bag Man. I just couldn't picture myself doing the things he did. Finally I got tired and went upstairs.

As I got undressed I walked around to my wife's side of the bed. I just stood there staring at her. She was already asleep. She was so beautiful and had a peaceful smile on her face. I think she already knew what I was going to do. I'm glad one of us did! How did I get so lucky to have such a wonderful wife? When I got into bed, still asleep, she instinctively rolled over and cuddled next to me, laying her arm across my chest. Knowing she was at peace made me feel peaceful also.

day

FIFTEEN

When I woke the next morning, it seemed like I had been through a two-week-long dream. But it wasn't a dream; it was real. It was Monday again, the beginning of a new week. I felt like I had changed some, yet I was still the same person. I couldn't put into words how I felt. I just knew that somehow things were different.

I could hear the kids in the background getting ready for the last week of school. The familiar smell of Elizabeth's cooking filled the air. As wonderful as it was, it was still the same old routine. How was that going to change my life and my destiny? I didn't know.

After breakfast our day continued as it normally did, and off to work I went. It was difficult to concentrate on what I was doing. My mind kept going back to the letter from the Bag Man. I had to refocus my mind several times. As expected, it was a very difficult day for me. I just couldn't understand what the Bag Man saw in me.

When I left work that day, I went straight home. I didn't even want to go to the square for my exercise. I didn't want to deal with the mental stress from knowing the Bag Man wouldn't be there. A few days off from exercise would give my body time to rest and recover. That was the excuse I used.

When I arrived home Elizabeth greeted me at the door.

"I never did get that dinner you promised me Friday morning. The kids are doing their homework and eating with the neighbors. We are going out for dinner. I want to go to the steak house on the square."

"Okay, whatever you want, dear."

As we were being seated by the hostess from the restaurant, we noticed that Sarah and Ronald Willingham was already seated with another couple just a few tables down from us. They recognized us and waved. We enjoyed a nice dinner alone without the kids. Conversation was good, and we didn't even bring up the Bag Man at all.

We weren't trying to be nosey, but we couldn't help but overhear some of what the Willinghams were talking about. They were telling their friends about what happened to them, and how the Bag Man gave them courage to work things through. They had already finished eating their meal and were just sitting there drinking their coffee and talking. After a few minutes Ronald got up and excused himself from his table and came over to where we were sitting.

"Hi, Peter, hi, Elizabeth, how are you guys doing?"

"Just having a quiet night out without the kids," Elizabeth said.

I nodded in agreement and then commented, "I see that you and Sarah are out with friends tonight. That's good."

"Yes that is great!" he said. "They are some long time friends of ours that we haven't seen in a while. They were passing through town on business and decided to give us a call at the last minute."

Elizabeth took a drink and interrupted, "Yes, it's wonderful to have long time friends you can count on and have no problems being yourself around. You know, people you don't have to be careful with or wear a mask around. You can just be you without any reservations."

"Exactly!" he said. "That is why I came over to your table just now. They are special friends to us and live the same lifestyle as Sarah and me. I know for a fact that they are going through some marital problems similar to what Sarah and I have been going through. We were just talking with them about how the Bag Man helped us realize what to do. We are trying to help them get through their problems too."

"That is fantastic!" I replied.

"Well, I'm not so sure about that. Sarah and I still have some of our own issues to work out, but we are on the right path. I was wondering if sometime in the near future Sarah and I could meet with you and talk about how we can help others that are going through the same problems that we are going through."

I looked over at Elizabeth, and she nodded her head 'yes.'

"We would be happy to," I said. "But let me be clear with you. We are not licensed counselors, but we will help as much as possible."

"That's great!" Ronald said. "Thank you so much. When can we meet?"

I again looked at Elizabeth. Without even skipping a beat she replied, "We are free tomorrow night."

"Great. I'll have Sarah call you later to work out the details. You guys really don't know how much you are helping us. Thanks again. See you tomorrow night."

Ronald walked back over to his own table and continued talking to his friends. I looked back again at Elizabeth and said, "I feel like we need to help them, but I'm not exactly sure what to say to them."

Elizabeth reached across the table and took both of my hands in hers and said, "We'll just share with them what we do in our relationship. We don't have to be perfect we just have to be real."

When we left the restaurant, we started walking around the square, just to relax. What we witnessed on the square that night will forever be etched in our souls. As we walked around for a bit we saw several of our new friends we made the night before.

There was Tiffany. She was there with Brandi Collins, the former drug addict. They were talking with some of Tiffany's friends. One of them was thinking about running away with her boyfriend. They were telling her what they had been through and giving her positive advice about what to do and what not to do. They told her that everything was not as it seemed.

As we continued to walk we saw Harry standing at the corner on the other side of the road. He waved as we passed by. He was a little preoccupied with another gentleman. It looked like he was giving him something to eat. He was telling his story while the guy ate his food and listened. I think it was one of his friends. At least he acted like it.

As we made our way around the square to the side streets we ran into John and Margaret Avery. We stopped and were talking with them when all of a sudden somebody came up to us from behind and put a hat on my head. It was John's father, Charles. He greeted us and then walked away toward a stack of boxes on the corner of the square. I pulled the hat from my head and looked at it. It was just a simple, inexpensive, white hat that had the words "Bag Man" printed on the front of it.

Margaret said, "Don't worry about him. Lately, he's been acting like a kid in a candy store. He even bought a supply of hats and had 'Bag Man' printed on the front of them. He's been giving them away for free to anyone who wanted one. Occasionally, he gets to tell the story about the Bag Man. He said it was his way of doing ministry. We are so proud of him!"

John spoke and said, "Dad said he had a new purpose in life and it made him feel young again."

We walked back around the square until we found ourselves almost back where we started. As we got closer to the other side, we saw a group of people, about ten or so, sitting and talking. We assumed they were sitting on the benches. It wasn't until we had a clearer view that we realized everyone was sitting in wheelchairs. One familiar person was sitting in front and everyone else was gathered around him. It was Terry Wells, the former wheelchair guy. He was conducting a meeting of some kind about how to make life better for yourself while in a wheelchair.

We continued walking our way back to our vehicle, which took us back toward the restaurant where we ate. We saw the Willinghams as they were leaving the restaurant. They parted from their friends and met us on the sidewalk. They were excited because they believed they would be able to help their friends with their marriage problems.

While standing there on the sidewalk I noticed a flyer posted in the window of the restaurant. I pointed it out to the others. It was a flyer advertising the start of a youth program involving sports events for handicapped children. More specifically, wheelchair handicapped children. Anyone interested in getting involved needed to contact instructor Terry Wells at a certain phone number.

About that time, Terry Wells walked up behind us and said, "I see you found one of the flyers I posted."

I asked, "What are you trying to accomplish by doing this?"

He simply said, "I'm not sure, I'm just trying to keep a promise I made to someone special."

Ronald joined the conversation, "What did you have in mind?"

"Well, I haven't worked out all of the details yet, but I'd like to try to make a difference in the lives of people with wheelchair handicaps, and maybe have programs for all youth and children. Maybe, if I can get them involved and off the streets, they will turn out to be leaders for the cause. I also want to start a wheelchair basketball league. It will help them with their self-confidence. I've been there. They need it a lot."

"What kind of financial backing do you have?"

"I don't have any. I'll have to raise most of the money myself. The county Department of Recreation will help out some, but it will be a slow process to start with."

"I'd like to help out. Here is my business card. Call my secretary and set up an appointment with me. I want to talk with you about funding your program. I think it's a worthy cause and needs to be handled correctly."

"I don't care who is in charge of it as long as I get to keep my promise and help other people."

"No, no. I don't want to be in charge. This is your baby, and you need to be in control. I just want to help out any way I can."

"I'll call your secretary tomorrow then."

"Great!"

As Terry walked away from us, Sarah spoke with a surprised look on her face.

"Did I hear you correctly? You, my husband, the successful business man who only deals with multimillion-dollar business deals, wants to help with something small like this. What gives?"

"I'm trying to make some changes in my life. I want to help him fulfill his promise and his dream. Besides, if it makes a difference in one person's life, it's all ready a big deal!"

When we reached our car to go home, I first unlocked the passenger's door for my wife, then I went to the driver's side. When I opened the door I hesitated and looked back toward the square. *What did I witness here tonight?* My mind was still full of questions that I had no answers for. Instinctively I turned my eyes toward heaven and began to question God. I've heard people say in the past that God talked to them in their spirits, or God spoke to their hearts. Some would say they just knew in their minds what God said because He doesn't speak in an audible voice. It didn't happen that way for me. I actually heard God speak with my own ears. I actually carried on a conversation with God. It scared me a little because I wasn't expecting a reply so soon or in that manner, or even at all.

"God, I need to hear from you."

"What do you need, Peter?"

"I need some answers."

"What are your questions?"

"All of the things that have happened over the last two weeks, did it really happen or is this a dream?"

"It really happened."

"Was the Bag Man real?"

"Yes."

"Are you the Bag Man?"

"Does it matter?"

"Yes, I need to know."

"Why?"

"I need to know before I make any decisions that affect my future and the future of my family."

"If you must know, the answer is yes and no."

"I don't understand."

"My ways are higher than your ways, so you will never understand completely. The Bag Man was an ambassador of mine. I chose him to represent me on earth. He did my work and spoke my words. Everything he did or said came from me. He was an extension of me. I was with him and in him. So, in a sense, it was me."

"Why did he choose me to finish his work?"

"He chose you because I told him to."

"Then why did *you* choose me?"

"I chose you because I saw a willing heart inside of you."

"Why did the Bag Man have to die?"

"Because his time on earth was complete and he finished the tasks that I gave him. His two main objectives were to help people in your community and to recruit you to take his place."

"I don't have the skills to take his place."

"I will give you the skills you need."

"But still, I'm not the Bag Man."

"I'm not asking you to be him. I'm asking you to fulfill the destiny I have planned for you. Look around the square. These people are eager to do my work, but they are like newborn babies. They need a leader to guide them the correct way. They need your help. Will you be their leader?"

"I'm afraid I might not do a good job."

"Fear not. As I was with and in the Bag Man, so shall I be with you. Will you fulfill the destiny I have planned for you?"

"Yes. Yes I will."

———

As I sat down in the seat of the car, Elizabeth asked me what I said. She said she thought I said something as I was getting into the car. I just nodded my head, acknowledging that I heard her. She tried to carry on a conversation during the drive home, but it was obvious to her that I had other things on my mind.

As Elizabeth lay in my arms that night she asked me why I was so preoccupied. I told her about the conversation I had with God. She sat up and focused on every word that God said to me. She said it was important to be specific about the exact words God used. Apparently it meant something to her also.

As we lay back down in each other's arms she asked, "How are we planning on accomplishing this task He has for us?"

"I don't know. I guess we'll just have to trust God on this one."

"Wow, trusting God. That's a novel idea. That sounds like something the Bag Man would say!"